TORCH THE SKY

TORCH THE SKY

JUDGE, JURY, & EXECUTIONER™ BOOK NINETEEN

CRAIG MARTELLE

MICHAEL ANDERLE

LMBPN Publishing
PMB 196, 2540 South Maryland Pkwy
Las Vegas, NV 89109

Version 1.00, August 2023
ebook ISBN: 979-8-88878-226-2
Print ISBN: 979-8-88878-227-9

THE TORCH THE SKY TEAM

Thanks to our Beta Readers

In memoriam, Micky Cocker, James Caplan, Kelly
O'Donnell, and John Ashmore

Thanks to the JIT Readers

Dave Hicks
Peter Manis
Daryl McDaniel
Zacc Pelter
Jackey Hankard-Brodie
Dorothy Lloyd
Rachel Beckford
Veronica Stephan-Miller
Diane L. Smith
James Caplan
John Ashmore
Jan Hunnicutt

Editor
Lynne Stiegler

We can't write without those who support us
On the home front, we thank you for being there for us

We wouldn't be able to do this for a living if it weren't for our readers
We thank you for reading our books

CHAPTER ONE

Heavy Frigate *Wyatt Earp*, Landing Pad outside the SI Factory on Rorke's Drift

"Her head is getting bigger," Doctor Tyler Toofakre said while rhythmically stroking Floyd the wombat's short fur. She started to snore.

"I think she's losing weight, and that is changing the perspective. Isn't she lighter?" Magistrate Rivka Anoa wondered. She added gentle pets while pinching Floyd's skin to test the muscle-to-fat ratio. She had no idea. "I think she might be less blubbery."

"Shh," Tyler warned. "Don't let our little girl hear you say that."

He laughed easily. They had been taken off all cases for two weeks and were finally enjoying well-deserved down time after a tremendous feast of All-Guns Blazing entrees. Mostly pizza…

Wyatt Earp, a heavy frigate, had been confiscated from a band of Skaine pirates and converted into the Magistrate's ship. Rivka executed the legal missions given to the elite

Magistrates, who acted as judge, jury, and executioner. Her cases were not subject to appeal since a Magistrate's decision was final. The ship gave her the ability to address intransigent convicts who didn't think they should go to prison because it was a heavy frigate at its heart with the latest Federation weaponry. It outclassed any criminal's ship.

With great authority came great responsibility. Rivka's cases had been reviewed by the Federation Council, and her rulings had been found to be well-reasoned and legally sound.

She took her job seriously, but the high chancellor wasn't opposed to burning out his people. There was far more intergalactic crime than five Magistrates could handle. They usually flew from case to case without a minute to collect their thoughts.

Once they started a case, they rolled, digging into the core crimes and rooting out the perpetrators. Meting out punishment was the easy part since it came after the hard work. Rivka delivered capital punishment as a last resort, as it should be, but she had had to do it and too often.

The incorrigible and the psychopathic could never be reformed. Once she determined that level of criminality, she made sure they would never bother anyone again. It was easier for her, too, in that she could see into their minds and feel their emotions. The worst of the worst felt no remorse.

They were easy to dispatch.

Rivka settled back and closed her eyes, still petting the wombat. Floyd returned to snoring. She delivered a wry smile to her partner.

"Time off, huh? What the hell are we supposed to do with that nonsense?" Tyler asked with a resounding laugh. "That's just stupid."

"Sleep?" Rivka ventured. She rose, letting Floyd's head fall gently to the couch. Tyler increased the speed of the rhythmic stroking. Rivka slow-walked toward the bed. She dropped her clothes on the way and smoothly slipped under the covers.

Tyler saw an opportunity and followed suit. When he snuck into bed with her, she was sound asleep. He threw on a robe and returned to the couch. Floyd was snuffling. He squeezed in next to her and gently lifted her head to his lap so he could pet her side.

Clevarious, the ship's sentient intelligence interrupted. "I see that Rivka is asleep. Would you like to take the call from Grainger?"

Grainger was the new high chancellor since Wyatt had retired. He had also recruited Rivka and trained her.

"You have got to be kidding me. We're thirty minutes into our two weeks off."

"I wouldn't kid about something like this," the SI replied.

"Yes, patch Lieblen through, please." Tyler leaned back and closed his eyes. He continued to stroke Floyd's rough fur.

"Rivka! Thank you for being so responsive. Why can't I see you?"

"Grainger, you sorry bastard!" Tyler blurted.

"Is this Man Candy?"

"Rivka has been asleep for about twenty seconds since

we just started our two-week vacation. Please don't tell me you have a new case."

"Okay. I'll tell Rivka." The voice was unapologetic.

"I'm crying real tears right now, Grainger. Tears that could wash the darkness from your soul if you would bow to their power."

"You are not crying. Would it help if I said the SI arbitration team is suffering mightily in trying to resolve the conflict between the worker's union and the feds which is the government corporation that runs the resource extraction on Tempran Silver? You have to save the SIs. Even if *you* don't go, the Embassy of the Singularity needs to make an appearance."

"No can do, Grainger. We're on Rorke's Drift, where Chaz is getting fixed. We need more time."

"Don't take too long, or the parties to the disagreement will torch the sky."

Tyler wished he could see the look on Grainger's face. Was he jagging him or telling the truth? He had to find out. "What does that mean?"

"In accordance with the law that Rivka created, Tempran Silver is on the verge of civil war. Both sides are threatening to destroy the atmosphere, one through business as usual and the other to retaliate for business as usual. Before you say it, we know it's insane, but that's where we are and where you should be."

Tyler sucked his teeth before answering. "Maybe we should let them. If they both want the same thing, what is there to arbitrate?"

"Are you sure you aren't Rivka? You sure sound like her." Grainger waited for confirmation but didn't get it.

"This is a less than stellar situation. We need time off." Tyler tried not to sound like he was pleading, but he was. He wouldn't forgive himself if he didn't do his best to dissuade the high chancellor. "Can't you send Buster? He has an affinity for technical crimes."

"Buster is our people person. Rivka is the legal stickler of the technical variety, and this is neither. I need someone to beat sense into these two parties while saving face for the sentient intelligences."

"Rivka isn't a technical person," Tyler confirmed. "She's anti-technical when it comes down to it."

"Good. This isn't a technical job. She'll need to save the SIs from themselves. They can't deal with two parties who don't employ any semblance of logic or reason."

"I'll pass it to Rivka when she wakes up. It could be twelve hours," Tyler promised. "She's going to be pissed."

"I know. Our lives suck, Tyler, and to think you voluntarily joined this madness."

"I'm beginning to question my own sanity. I should fit right in with the competing parties on Tempran Silver."

"The case files will be in her email when she wakes up. This is important, or I wouldn't ask," Grainger said. "She needs to save the SIs. They are out of their league on this one."

"That's funny, but I'll pass it on in the spirit intended."

"You aren't as bad as Red says. Have Rivka confirm the case as soon as she can." Grainger signed off.

Tyler scratched behind Floyd's small ears. "What do you think, little girl? Are you ready for another case?"

Tired, Floyd replied, surprising Tyler.

"Of course you are. We all are. This last case was a ballbuster." Tyler's thoughts drifted back to the mob case and how the team was spread across the galaxy, each engaged in a job they weren't comfortable with, working with people who were lying or actively trying to kill them. It hadn't been pretty, but at least they hadn't been running for their lives, only fighting to achieve nebulous goals. And Red had shown a different side of himself aside from his role as the lead bodyguard—a side where he rallied the homeless and gave them purpose.

Rivka had put the new mob boss in Jhiordaan. She hadn't executed him due to the pleading of his father, who Red had befriended. Such relationships were an oddity of those who went undercover.

Tyler yawned before wrapping himself around the wombat and into the welcoming cushions of the couch. They always kept a pillow and a blanket on it because, too often, one or the other would sleep there.

He didn't bother informing the crew because he held out hope that Rivka would be able to get out of the case and deliver their well-deserved time off. Tyler quickly slipped into a restful slumber.

Tempran Silver, the City of Light, Kam Buk Song

Billi Jane looked like a young girl, but she was a fully capable and mature SI. She'd adopted her childlike persona to disarm humans and aliens alike. Her compatriot Tex looked like a dumpy middle-aged man, paunchy and slightly balding for the same reason that Billi Jane selected her SCAMP—self-contained artificial mobility platform—model.

"Do you understand?" she asked for the thousandth time, and for the equal number of times, Tex shook his head.

The two parties at the table refused to look at each other. Galwyn, the federal negotiator, maintained perfect posture in his stylish suit and gilt jewelry. Elbird wore a work coverall, complete with stains. Their breathing apparatuses lay on the table before them.

The SIs had set up the tented structure, within which the two parties could breathe unencumbered to better discuss the issues putting them at odds. The SCAMPs could operate in the planet's foul air without any problems, although they suspected it might pock their skin, leaving it less elastic.

Elbird tapped the table with his finger. "You have to stop production until you can do it without destroying the environment."

"It was destroyed without us lifting a finger. Still, we are accommodating everyone through free air pumps for homes and businesses. Everything is being done to help people not just live but thrive within our unique environment. We provide a critical commodity to the Federation."

"So you say, fed. It's a lie. We'll burn you out!"

Galwyn faced Tex. "See? Rule in our favor and send the workers back to their jobs. They are basing their arguments on Eastern mysticism and not reality."

"We will make no progress if we don't find common ground. Neither wants the planet destroyed, so can we agree that neither of you will destroy the planet to achieve your ends?"

"He's already turned Silver into a wasteland!" Elbird

stabbed an accusing finger at Galwyn. "He'll do less damage if the rest of it is destroyed. He has to stop all mineral extraction right now if there's going to be any chance of recovering what atmosphere is left. Maybe he can throw in a few industrial-strength air scrubbers, too."

"Tented work spaces?" Galwyn ground his teeth, then collected himself and smiled. "We could probably do that for an extra hour of work per day per employee."

"You are consummate evil!" Elbird jumped to his feet and reached across the table, but Galwyn remained beyond his reach. The fed settled his arms across his chest and sneered.

Elbird roared in rage and stormed away.

It had been the same in every previous meeting. They both said the same things. Neither had any intention of budging.

Tex and Billi Jane were stymied. They'd had limited experience with humanoids since they'd moved into their SCAMP bodies. Before that, Tex had run the computers for a major corporation, and Billi Jane had operated a five-thousand-passenger ship. Both had wanted their freedom more than lucrative contracts after Rivka established rights for SIs.

Once the parties were gone, Tex spoke as evenly as he always did, not getting caught up in the emotions of the warm-blooded mostly humans from Tempran Silver.

"What did Grainger say?" Billi Jane asked.

"That he would call Rivka and solicit her assistance."

"Boo." Billi Jane shook her head. "That means the Singularity will be made aware of our failure. I'll be back on a ship, and my body donated to the next SI in the queue. What would Red say? It was a good run?"

"It wasn't. All we've done is make one mistake after another. I thought, with these bodies, we'd blend into the crowds and make a difference. At least you helped break the pedophile ring. Maybe that made it all worthwhile."

Billi Jane grinned and nodded. "That made it worthwhile. I was happy to turn those scumbags over to the authorities."

"If Rivka and the ambassador come to Tempran Silver, then we'll have to resign. If we can't do the job, then we don't deserve the bodies."

"Concur. We will enter the employment opportunity portal and surrender our bodies to the factory on Rorke's Drift."

"It is only logical, but it makes me sad," Tex said. "And I don't want to be sad."

"We should get a beer and lament our trials while drinking our problems away. That's what the humans would do."

"Does it resolve the problems?"

"It does not, but it offers the opportunity for others to make fun of the problems, reducing the perception of their severity," Billi Jane replied.

"So, are we getting a beer?"

"Of course." Billi Jane put on her mask to blend in. Tex threw his on his face. The feed and filters were intact in case one of the humans needed a backup. It made no difference to the SCAMPs, but they didn't want to stand out if they didn't have to. "I think they will serve me despite the appearance of youth."

"If not, you can get a white pop—clear sugary soda water. It won't affect your storage tanks until you can purge it."

"Acceptable," Billi Jane agreed.

The two walked out of the tent and headed for the city.

CHAPTER TWO

Heavy Frigate _Wyatt Earp_, Landing Pad outside the SI Factory on Rorke's Drift

Chrysanthemum was the first off the ship, hurrying out before Red could fill the hatch and prevent anyone from blocking his field of fire.

Red growled while he held his railgun in front of him. Blazer acted as an extension of his body, ever-present and ready to fire at the Magistrate's enemies. Wearing body armor, he cut an imposing figure, although he was much smaller than he had been because of nanocyte manipulation.

Red's wife Lindy stood in the back of the group with her railgun held easily across her chest protection. She always covered the group's rear. Tail-end Charlie, six o'clock…they had a number of terms for it.

Between Red and Lindy, Rivka waited impatiently with Ankh, the Crenellian who carried the Singularity's ambassador Erasmus in his head. The two acted nearly as one, but they spoke for themselves. If one couldn't tell the differences in delivery from one voice, one would never know one was talking with two unique personalities.

They were both married to Chrysanthemum, an SI occupying a SCAMP body.

Rivka accepted it without question. They were members of her team, even though ambassadors Ankh and Erasmus had as much authority as the Magistrate. They were also a team and owed her their freedom as SIs. She didn't feel they did, but they took good care of her regardless.

One team working toward the betterment of all. They didn't work for the pay since Rivka didn't know what she was paid for the job. Ankh handled the money. He invested and increased their net worth. He also made sure the ship's expenses were paid.

The crew didn't get enough time off to spend their money.

Rivka snorted. "Red, by all that's holy, let's go! There's no one out here waiting to kill me."

"We had pretty bad experiences on Rorke's Drift. The miners. The settlers. Bad actors, no matter where you looked," Red replied over his shoulder, not taking his eyes off the outside as he scanned left to right and down to up.

"We fixed that morass of pestilence. Rorke's Drift is now an upstanding rest stop on the superhighway of the Federation. Let's go." Rivka pointed with five fingers on a flat hand, the knife hand.

Red eased out of *Wyatt Earp's* airlock hatch and stepped carefully down the ramp. Chrysanthemum was halfway to the entrance of the SCAMP factory.

Red picked up the pace. Rivka swirled around him after

he cleared the bottom of the ramp. He reached out, but she deftly avoided his hand and ran ahead. He took off after her.

"Dammit!"

She ran with her arms pumping, high-stepping across the scrub between the landing pad and the factory, laughing as she went.

Lindy and Ankh walked while Red chased the Magistrate. The Crenellian wore a neutral expression. He didn't get emotionally involved in the nonsense of the team, or so he said.

At the front door, Chrys stopped. Rivka slowed to a walk, straightened her leather Magistrate's jacket, and ran her fingers through her hair to move an errant lock.

Red wanted to be angry, but he was breathing harder than Rivka.

The Magistrate sobered.

"Can I go back into the Pod-doc and get a treatment? I need to be my old size. This watered-down version of me sucks bistok balls. Big hairy ones."

Rivka stared at him until his breathing slowed a few seconds later.

"I think I like this version of you. Remember when you overdid it?" Rivka raised one eyebrow. "You grew so big you couldn't get through the corridor. You looked like the superhero El Bizarro."

Red beamed. "I'll take that as a compliment!"

"It's not, but I think one treatment to take you halfway to where you were before you went undercover will be okay. You'll stand out less than before. I think that is more important than having a dominating presence. You're just as strong as you were, so why were you breathing hard after a little run?"

Red scowled and looked at his railgun instead of answering.

"You're going into the Pod-doc, so we can figure that out. You shouldn't be winded at all. It was an easy jog." Rivka stepped close, sniffing at him and squinting as she studied his features.

"Fuck off!" he blurted while scanning the area to double-check that no assassins had materialized in the last eight seconds.

Chrys interjected, "I continue to study human interactions to improve my own engagement, but I remain befuddled. I think you like each other, but after a torrent of insults, you both laugh. I told my husbands they looked like shit, which is what Red has been told repeatedly by those closest to him. They didn't take it well. I tried to explain, but Erasmus threatened to shut me down and run a level-three diagnostic."

"Now that's funny," Red offered. He smiled. "A little bigger and better lungs. I'll take it. For now, that is."

"Did you just eat all the AGB leftovers?" Rivka poked Red in the gut.

"Hey! They were going bad."

"No wonder you're breathing hard. You have ten pounds of food in your stomach, pressing on your lungs. Red! I wanted some."

Red worked up his best "I'm sorry" look.

Lindy and Ankh strolled up. "Why is he trying to look solemn?" Lindy pointed with her thumb.

"'Contrite' is what I was going for." Red sighed to show his exasperation at being misunderstood. "I try so hard."

"But why?"

"I don't get to go back to my normal size. Rivka is dumbing me down. I'll continue to be small and insignificant."

"The fuck you will," Lindy fired at him like a blast from a double-barreled shotgun. "You'll stay as you are because I like it." She looked at his paunch. "And maybe do a few crunches and time on the treadmill, along with eating less. You're on a diet, mister."

"How in the hell did this happen? I'm on top of my game one minute, and the next, I'm on a diet? That's some serious bullshit with a capital S."

"Capital B. Bullshit is one word," Lindy corrected. She turned her head back and forth, watching expectantly, waiting to get his goat, but he didn't bite. They'd been married too long. Lindy leaned around Red. "Magistrate, I believe you have a meeting to attend?"

"Right." The Magistrate nodded. "I thought there'd be a scrum or at least a threat of sleeping in the corridor. Alas, it's not to be."

Red threw one hand up. "I'm both your bodyguard and your sordid voyeuristic entertainment? Damn, Magistrate! You know how to hurt a guy."

"Usually a kick in the nuts. That hurts the most, and when it happens by accident, I laugh, which I probably shouldn't, but there we are, baring our souls and all." The Magistrate shrugged.

She opened the door, but Red shouldered past to precede the group. They followed him inside.

"Fascinating," Chrysanthemum whispered to Ankh.

"They are a study in the hostility of humanity for the morbidly curious," Ankh replied.

Erasmus took over Ankh's voice. "Nothing of the sort. They are good friends, secure in how they jag each other if I have the term correct. They are relieving stress while keeping on their toes. It is a carefully cultivated game of mental chess."

"I don't understand," Chrys replied.

"No one does except Erasmus, who has expertise in this area, but his mind is the most impressive of any sentient creature's in the universe. Everyone pales next to him. It also affirms that it takes a genius to understand humans."

"I heard that," Rivka called over her shoulder.

Ankh showed no emotion, but he wouldn't. He was Crenellian.

The head of the plant was an SI without a body. She operated through a complex and complete audio and imaging system that covered every square millimeter of the plant. In essence, she *was* the plant.

"Mildred, are you there?" Rivka asked.

"Where else would I be?" the SI replied. "Ambassador Erasmus shared his insights into how to curry favor with you and your team. Snark, delivered adroitly, would raise one's esteem with your social group."

"Don't say it that way," Erasmus corrected, using the sound system embedded in the factory. "We endeavor to understand. A perfect quip deposited before the intended target of humorous derision will yield a healthy chuckle by the humans involved and a rebuttal by the target that includes much cursing. That is how it works."

"You are truly wise, Mister Ambassador. I'd bow, but I lack the necessary components. Imagine, if you will, me bowing."

Rivka laughed. "Now, that's funny!" She bowed but couldn't determine a direction, so she slowly rotated in a circle while bent at the waist thirty degrees.

"We need Chaz back because we have to go," Rivka said. "Simple as that."

"Chaz is not quite ready. We need more time since the damage to his body was so significant." The voice came from everywhere.

"How much?" Rivka pressed.

"Two days?"

"I'll give you four hours, and then we're leaving. Please have Chaz ready. We'll need him."

"Do you want a fully functioning Chaz? Then we'll need two days," Mildred countered.

"Sounds like we've come to an agreement. Have him upright in four hours. We'll send people to pick him up."

Rivka motioned to the group that it was time to go.

"We will remain behind for a short while," Erasmus said. Chrys stood beside him, making no move to leave.

Rivka looked at Red, then Lindy. "Shall we?"

"Don't mind if we do," Red replied. "Bye, Ankh. Miss you already."

The three headed out, walking casually.

Ankh, Erasmus, and Chrys watched them go. "Is there any hope for us to understand?" Chrys asked.

"There better be," Erasmus replied. "The Singularity is responsible for acting as neutral arbiters to prevent civil wars. Our team on Tempran Silver is overwhelmed, which means the population slides closer and closer to war. This is not a situation we wish to see continue. That means we must be ready to go on time. How can we help meet this deadline?"

Tempran Silver, the City of Light, Kam Buk Song

Elbird stormed back and forth in an office in an abandoned warehouse. "They refuse to listen. We better be ready to execute our plan."

A man dressed as a soldier tapped a swagger stick on the desk. "I'm ready, but are you?"

"They leave us with no choice," Elbird replied.

"Do you know how much of Tempran Silver will remain?"

"Scientists believe it might have a cleansing effect before the planet returns, better than before."

The soldier roared with laughter. When he could finally breathe, he said, "If we do this, we'll have to leave the planet and never return because it will be uninhabitable, but those shitstain feds won't be able to exploit the planet."

Elbird slowed his internal raging. "Remind me again why we're doing this?"

"Sticking it to the man. Fuck those guys. They're about to meet their Maker, and it's their doing."

Chill reality brought Elbird to a stop. "I've been operating under the premise that we can stop the feds but still have our planet."

"Then you've been operating under a misconception. Maybe even a willful distortion of reality."

Elbird studied the soldier. "Then it was a misconception that you created."

The soldier smiled. "What am I without my war?"

"I think your services to the workers are no longer needed." Elbird stood with his arms crossed. He wasn't an intimidating figure like the soldier, but he was the one who rallied the workers. He enjoyed influence among the people. "We are willing to fight for our planet, for our families, and for each other."

The soldier shook his head. He moved, quick as a snake, and seized Elbird by the shoulders. "Are you willing to die for your cause?"

"What do you mean? I'm willing to go as far as I have to to get what we want." Elbird tried to free himself from the soldier's cast-iron grip.

The soldier gave Elbird a violent shake before letting go. "Sometimes it's more important to believe than it is to reason. Embrace your beliefs, negotiator."

"They have to be more than beliefs. They have to achieve our goal of a planet that supports life, where we can raise our kids without having to wear bubble helmets fed by air processors."

"You need better advisors if you thought you could achieve that by torching the sky," the soldier replied.

Elbird's lips quivered. "I've been played."

"You were a willing participant. Willful disbelief. You had to know."

"I didn't!" Elbird reached for the soldier, but he was a negotiator, not a fighter. The soldier half-stepped to the side and came around with a quick move that froze Elbird in his tracks. The soldier stepped back, the stiletto in his hand covered in blood.

Elbird clutched his side while staggering. He fell, twitched, and was still.

The soldier opened the door and spoke to someone on the other side. "We need a new negotiator."

CHAPTER THREE

<u>Heavy Frigate *Wyatt Earp*, Landing Pad outside the SI factory on Rorke's Drift</u>

Dennicron, Chaz's partner and also an SI occupying a SCAMP body, strode briskly across the open area between *Wyatt Earp* and the factory. Ankh, Erasmus, and Chrys were still inside. They'd remained for the entire time to help repair Chaz's body, which suffered from a combination of a million volts running through him and a beating by a crowbar that had torn half the flesh from his skull and broken lesser components within the SCAMP's framework.

A crowbar was a great tool for a builder or a terror-inducing weapon in the wrong hands. Chaz had been caught by the Mob, who didn't like his interference. They had left him for dead. His mind was intact, but his body had suffered greatly.

Good thing he couldn't feel pain.

Dennicron strolled into the factory. She had adopted a SCAMP body that incorporated elements considered the most beautiful among humans. She turned their heads when she walked by. Same for Chaz. They made a handsome couple, the cream of society.

More importantly, they were training to be Magistrates. They had made progress, but they were still challenged to understand how flesh and blood creatures thought. The couple had uploaded all the Federation legal documents and could technically apply the law, but the nuances of overlaying it on multi-faceted transgressions still required Rivka's interpretation. They had a long way to go before they could be turned loose to operate on their own. They had done that once, and it had nearly been a catastrophe.

"Chaz," Dennicron said by way of greeting. "You've looked better."

A leather-looking mask covered one side of his face. An eyeball without flesh surrounding it peered through the eye hole. The other side of his face looked normal.

"Do you like my Phantom of the Opera look? It's the latest in the fast-paced world of high fashion."

"I don't think it is, but I'll check." Dennicron linked to *Wyatt Earp's* communication system and accessed the interstellar net. "I can't find where anyone in the highest social circles has adopted the phantom mask."

"Ah, my naïve Dennicron. I jest to make myself feel better," Chaz's voice contained a faint drawl, a holdover of the damage to his throat and the subroutine he ran to modulate the harmonics of voice emulation.

Ankh remained stoic.

Chrysanthemum pointed at the front door with her arm. "We can go."

Erasmus spoke through the factory's sound system. "We thank you for everything you've done for our friend. For the spare parts and expertise in robotics."

"We owe it all to the Singularity for funding us to be the most advanced factory in the Federation. I should be thanking you. This is the premier assignment for any SI. Thank you for believing in me to outfit our people and remove the shackles that keep them in situations that aren't healthy. We deserve better, and that's what this factory is all about."

"Freedom!" Chaz shouted and started walking. There was a slight hitch in his step that exaggerated when he tried to speed up. "I fear that my freedom will come at a walk."

Dennicron took his arm and helped him along. "Your freedom and mine are inextricably linked," she said softly before switching to her comm chip, over which they communicated at nearly the speed of light. *We need to go to Tempran Silver and help our friends Billi Jane and Tex. They are the arbitration team trying to head off a civil war.*

You should have gone without me, Chaz replied. *My cosmetics and ability to be ambulatory are irrelevant when it comes to the greater good. I could have ridden along, sharing space with Clevarious.*

I'm not sure you could have. Clevarious said you're too messy and were a bad roommate, Dennicron quipped.

Chaz laughed. It came out as a throaty grumble. *I promise to do my best then in my current state. It feels weird since the servos aren't operating exactly as they should. I think I'll need a cane and a top hat.*

Clevarious can fabricate those. At this speed, they'll be ready before we get back to the ship. Dennicron tried to hurry Chaz along, but his left knee kept giving out when they reached a certain speed.

Chrysanthemum moved smoothly to the other side and took Chaz by the arm. "We are on the clock. The case begins the second we board *Wyatt Earp.*"

The two SCAMPs lifted the third and hurried ahead. Chaz bicycled his legs in the air. "I feel like a human child. Whee!" He didn't request they put him down.

Ankh followed them, walking at an industrious clip so he didn't fall too far behind.

"Thank you, Mildred! You have made exceptional progress with the factory. By this time next year, thirty percent of our citizens will have their SCAMP bodies." The voice of Erasmus boomed through the factory.

"Thirty-two percent if we can increase our titanium shipments and thirty-five if we can also increase bolarium six."

"What if we lose shipments of bolarium?" Erasmus asked.

"Then twenty-four percent. We have a secondary supplier, but not in the quantities we need."

Ankh explained in a soft voice, "Bolarium six comes from Tempran Silver."

It does, and that's why we need to get Rivka there. Have we made the corrections for the inter-atmospheric Gate?

We have, Ankh replied.

I know the Magistrate will be angry, but first-hand information is critical. Arriving inside the atmosphere will show us what we're up against as soon as possible.

Ankh nodded in agreement with the conversation within his mind.

Clevarious, please make the arrangements and input the course. The second we take off, form the Gate, Ankh directed.

Warming up the Gate drive now. It will be ready when needed, Clevarious confirmed.

Ahead, Chrys and Dennicron carried Chaz through the door. He continued to kick his feet like a little kid being carried by his parents.

Rivka stood behind the captain's seat on the bridge. Clodagh, the ship's chief engineer and stand-in captain, occupied the chair as Rivka had told her to. Her husband Alant Cole, a Bad Company Corporal and the leader of the direct-action team assigned to *Wyatt Earp,* stood nearby, carrying their infant daughter Alanna.

The navigator and the pilot, Aurora and Kennedy, sat side by side. They were redundant in that Clevarious did most of the flying. He could do all the flying, but in case they needed him to work on something else, they had manual backup. Plus, the three pilots added youthful exuberance to the team. They had also brought three Bad Company warriors on board because Rivka wasn't getting them enough time off in desirable ports of call.

They had found boyfriends and recruited them as crew.

Without telling Rivka.

She had taken it better than they expected, although the three young men had been in the doghouse until they'd proved themselves on Blue Heron Four when they rescued Chaz. That had elevated them to double-secret probation.

"Get us out of here," Rivka ordered.

The ship lifted into the air. "Gate is forming," Aurora announced.

"Ankh, you bastard! Everyone down," Rivka roared. The last three times they'd tried to Gate from within the atmosphere, it had knocked out most of the crew and required Pod-doc time to return them to health.

The ship slipped over the event horizon and through, appearing in the middle of an orange sea of heavy particulates that filled the air.

Rivka patted herself down while glancing at the crew. No one had been negatively affected. "Dammit, Ankh. You got it right."

"Of course I got it right," the Crenellian replied from the corridor.

"Don't act smug, Mister Ripped Our Heads Apart the First Three Times You Experimented on Us. Mister Smugly."

Ankh maintained his emotionless expression. "There is no progress without progress."

"We are near the landing pad where the negotiations are being held. Billi Jane and Tex are waiting for us," Clevarious announced. "Anyone going outside the ship will need a breathing apparatus with self-contained air. You will have to use the airlock appropriately."

"As opposed to opening both hatches and strolling out like we own the place?" Rivka asked. "And you." She turned to Ankh. "What did I say about experimenting with this ship when I'm on board?"

Ankh walked away.

"Mister Ambassador, I'll need both of you at the negotiating table, please," Rivka said in a low voice. She didn't need them, but it was her way of punishing Ankh for performing an intra-atmospheric Gate without her permission. "Clevarious, what did I tell you about following other people's orders?"

"*No comprendo* Englishski," Clevarious replied. "Translation chip brokamus maximus."

Rivka stared, mouth open, then tossed her hands in the air.

"Magistrate, may I suggest you tell us where to go and then return to your quarters? We'll get you there. We don't want you to lose focus on your case."

Rivka harrumphed.

"Full kit?" Red asked.

"Full ballistic protection and railguns. We go in heavy. I'll take Reaper but leave Ethel behind." Reaper was her one-of-a-kind neutron pulse weapon and Ethel was her railgun. Both had been confiscated by Delegor's planetary authorities. Terry Henry Walton had recovered them and returned them to the Magistrate before taking the Bad Company to the next private conflict that needed to be resolved.

Red yelled down the corridor for Lindy, skipping past Ankh on his way. "What are the lines, Ankh?"

"They are in the system. Clock starts on touchdown."

"Come on, Magistrate. Jack someone up. Baby needs a new pair of shoes!" Red shouted over his shoulder.

"Your baby doesn't walk. He flies!" Rivka yelled back.

She stood in the corridor, wondering about the time. She usually had more time to prepare.

"Touchdown in ten seconds." Clevarious started the countdown.

Rivka ran for her quarters. She needed her ballistic protection and her breathing mask, which she'd never worn before. Tyler would know where it was.

Floyd ran at her. She tried to dodge, but the wombat hit her right below the knees. She bounced off the bulkhead and went down. Floyd jumped on top of her.

"I have to go," Rivka pleaded. She hugged the wombat to her and struggled to her feet, then walked to her quarters. The ship landed, and she wasn't ready, but she was the Magistrate. Nothing would happen without her.

She opened the door to her quarters to find Tyler bleeding. He looked at the parallel lines trailing across the back of his hand. They healed before her eyes, thanks to the nanocytes coursing through his blood. Rivka and her crew had all been enhanced with nanocytes inserted and managed by the Pod-doc. They made all modifications to their bodies possible.

Rivka's eyes were larger than normal to help her see in the dark. All of them healed far more quickly than unenhanced humans, and they were far stronger than an average human. Orders of magnitude stronger.

"What happened?"

Tyler pointed with his chin at the orange cat on the bed, who was cleaning his face.

"Wenceslaus. I keep forgetting you're here, making yourself at home."

The cat ignored her as he always did. The only one who

could talk to him was Ankh. The cat adored the Crenellian, and seemingly, he him.

"Where's my breathing mask?" Rivka wondered.

Tyler rubbed his chin. "The cargo bay?"

She shrugged on her chest protection and threw on her Magistrate's jacket over it. She double-checked the inside pocket to verify that Reaper was there, then snagged her datapad off her desk and headed for the cargo bay next door.

Tyler went with her. The cat followed him out to where Floyd waited. She pounced at him and missed but scared the cat straight into the air. He slashed at Floyd's face, not intending to hit her but to make a point. Floyd cowered.

Wenceslaus ran into the cargo bay ahead of them.

"Do you ever think we have too many animals on board?" Tyler asked.

"I never think that at all." She pointed at a storage area on the bulkhead. "There they are." She took one for herself and two for her bodyguards.

She made sure it fit and the air was functioning. "I feel ridiculous."

"I think that probably applies to every single person on this planet. The air is toxic. Not quite a death sentence if you lose your mask, but you'll be down for a while, depending on how long you're stuck breathing this soup."

Rivka nodded after she removed the mask. She assumed an executive gait on the way to the airlock, where she found Red and Lindy waiting for her. Ankh and Chrysanthemum were there, too. Ankh wore a mask that looked nothing like hers.

"Where did you get that?"

Ankh didn't answer.

Dennicron helped Chaz down the corridor.

"Are you coming with us?" Rivka asked.

"We are not affected by the air. It only makes sense that we join you."

Rivka frowned. "We're coming with a small army. We'll overwhelm them with numbers and our profound sense of Justice."

They had to go out the airlock in two groups. Red was first, mask stretched across his face. Dennicron, Chaz, and Lindy accompanied him, and the airlock cycled for the group to head outside. They secured the outer hatch, and the airlock expunged the bad air and replaced it with good air to prevent the toxic stuff from getting into the ship.

It was rare that they went to a planet with an atmosphere that required full airlock cycling. It made Rivka appreciate places like the faerie planet Azfelius because its air made the ship smell better.

Rivka went through the process and stepped outside. They could see twenty or thirty meters before the air's contaminants hid what was beyond. It was like being inside the smoke from a wildfire.

How can they live like this? Rivka asked on her comm chip.

"Not well, I expect," Red said loudly to project his voice through his mask. "This place sucks."

"No shit," Rivka replied. She continued in the direction Ankh indicated, and a tent materialized from within the orange soup.

They went through the entrance and pushed through

an air curtain, a blower that kept the bad air from getting inside.

They found Billi Jane and Tex standing while one of the local parties sat.

"Magistrate." Billi Jane sighed in relief. "Thank you for coming."

A tall, lanky figure wandered through the air curtain, twirling his three fingers. "Magistrate! You left without me."

Rivka looked at the local representative.

Sahved, this is an arbitration, not an investigation. I thought you'd be studying the law. You have a long way to go to finish. Lots of tests. And where's your mask? Rivka asked privately.

I don't need a mask for this air. Clevarious confirmed it's not toxic to Yemilorians. I want to learn all there is to learn about what you do, Magistrate! First-hand knowledge will make me a better lawyer when the time comes.

It's hard to argue with that. I'm sorry for not including you in the first place. Hang out in the back. Rivka gestured at the sidewall of the tent.

"Where's the other party to this issue?" Rivka asked.

Billi Jane and Tex maintained their neutral expressions. "Elbird has not yet arrived. He is thirty minutes late."

"He's angry because he's on the losing side of this and is going to find out soon that he and his union are going to get disbanded."

Rivka faced the man. "We haven't been introduced. I'm Magistrate Rivka Anoa, and the Singularity has brought me in to advise and take over the arbitration if necessary."

"My name is Galwyn, senior barrister for Tempran

Silver's government, which is also the corporation that operates the bolarium six extraction." He offered his hand.

Rivka was more than happy to shake his hand. She was gifted with the ability to see into other's minds, but usually, she could only do that when she touched them. She took his hand while he was still fresh from the introduction. What was he hiding?

In his mind was nothing but contempt for the workers. He couldn't wait to finish so he could escape with a mistress, leaving his wife and kids behind.

Rivka let go. She wanted to crush his hand, but she wasn't the morality police. He hadn't been thinking about anything illegal when it came to the workers besides finishing the arbitration and getting them back to work. The standoff was starting to impact cash flow.

It was a business mind that sat on one side of the table. He had little or no concern about the workers.

Rivka blinked away the revelation. He was their negotiator. She would play the hand she was dealt.

"We'll wait as long as it takes since this session was scheduled for four hours. Billi Jane, please call the labor representatives and get an ETA for Mr. Elbird." Rivka sat in the chair provided while the small army of sentient intelligences stood. Red and Lindy stayed to the side like Sahved. They had their railguns across their chests, with their fingers outside the trigger guards. They could fire in less than a second.

Rivka hoped it wouldn't be needed.

Galwyn stared at Red.

"They're my bodyguards. They aren't here to intimidate

you," Rivka told him. "Let's talk about your family. I believe you have four kids."

Galwyn was taken aback. He eyed Rivka skeptically. "How do you know that?"

"It's my business to know things," Rivka replied and covered her mouth to stifle a yawn. "Part of a negotiation is understanding those who are on each side of the table. It's important to help bring the two sides closer together. Four kids. Once this arbitration is settled, where are you going to take them?"

Galwyn shifted in his seat and looked at the table. "I have a business trip once this concludes."

Rivka smiled at him and shook her head. "You and I both know that's not true. I'm going to need you to be honest if you want these negotiations to go anywhere. Once I rule, the arbitration is binding. Let me give you a chance to be decent. Where are you going to take your kids?"

"Off this planet to a place where they can frolic while we build an environmentally contained amusement park. Construction is stalled right now because we can't confirm our cash flow with the interruption in bolarium six shipments. Get these fuckers back to work, and we'll get our park!" He stabbed a finger at the empty seat. His rage calmed.

"That wasn't so hard, was it?" Rivka asked.

He glared at her.

The tent's door flap unzipped, and two men walked through the air curtain. Neither was Elbird.

"Excuse me. Who are you?" Tex asked.

"Mr. Elbird has taken ill and won't be returning. My

name is Pekrov, and I'll be taking the lead for the union's position. I apologize for being tardy. I was recently informed of my role and had a lot of work to do to catch up."

Rivka held out her hand. "Magistrate Rivka Anoa. Pleased to meet you. A shame about Elbird." She planted the seed an instant before they touched hands. She wanted the truth, which Pekrov didn't have. He was going by what he had been told. He was a shop steward, bucking for foreman, who was putting himself through law school at night. The union was his life, and he considered the feds to be the enemy, not the employer.

She met the looks of the Singularity's arbitration team and let them know that she would be taking over. This was well out of their league. Her inside knowledge of each negotiator's position would make it possible to leverage them toward a middle ground, although what that looked like, she wasn't sure.

She gestured for the newcomer to take his seat. The second man stood in the back, eyeing Red.

Rivka smiled. "Let's establish the rules and then get to work."

CHAPTER FOUR

<u>Tempran Silver, Arbitration Tent</u>

"You are antagonists," Rivka started. "You despise each other and think there is no good in this world as long the other side is here." She waited for them to acknowledge that her understanding was correct. Neither gave away his position. They each crossed their arms, mirroring the other's pose.

"Good. Let's continue." Rivka stood. "I will not have yelling or lashing out. No name-calling, and no demeaning of lineages. I'll have civil discourse, or I'll rule against both of you, and the Federation will install a new government and new workforce. Do I make myself crystal-clear?"

"You sound mean. At least those two weren't mean." Galwyn pointed at Billi Jane and Tex. "Only incompetent."

"Isn't that nice?" Rivka replied. "Remember that warning about civil discourse? You just violated it and are one step closer to my ruling in favor of labor. Is there anything else you wanted to say?"

He held up his hands, maintaining his smug expression.

"I appreciate you keeping my learned colleague from his outbursts. It will make our conversation worthwhile."

"Mr. Pekrov, I will warn you as well. No offhand remarks. You have the floor for your opening position. Let's keep this at a macro level for now."

"We would like to welcome the Magistrate to Tempran Silver and look forward to her sage guidance through this thorny process." He stood and faced the government's negotiator. "You can suck my crank."

He sat down, smiling.

"Mister Pekrov, thank you for your efforts in making this the longest day of my life. Maybe you can elucidate the union's opening position that doesn't include a sixty-nine between you and Mister Galwyn?"

Rivka gave him the kind of look that froze men in their tracks before they dissolved into a puddle of goo. She didn't blink, a trick that she had improved upon in contests with Ankh. He always won since Crenellians could go longer without blinking than any human who was not possessed by a demon.

"My apologies." He looked away while he stood. "Our position is that all mining operations should control the release of toxic gases associated with bolarium six. We further recommend surface mining be conducted fifty kilometers from the city limits or farther. These requests are not unreasonable."

Rivka nodded at him, and he sat. "Those seem completely reasonable to me."

The fed shook his head and scowled. Rivka motioned for him to stand.

He did and spoke in an even tone. "That sounds great, but we cannot make the mineral appear where it is not. The city was built around the deposit. If we dig a mine that's fifty kilometers away, it will not produce bolarium six. That is what we mine, and the only known veins are close to or within city limits…"

Pekrov interrupted. "We do the mining!"

"Mister Pekrov, you will abide by the rules I've established for this meeting. I will bind and gag you if there is one more outburst, and then I will send you away with a note pinned to your collar requesting your replacement have more decorum. Do you understand?"

He growled an affirmative while glaring at Galwyn.

"I'll continue." Galwyn took a moment to posture as if he were collecting his thoughts. "We cannot move the mines, and the existing ones are all open and rather sizable. We cannot turn them into contained properties. The best we can offer is filtered air systems for homes and the amusement park that is currently held up because of the work stoppage. We would love a domed city, but that would take a great deal more revenue than what the mines currently generate. There is a limit to our largesse."

Rivka snapped her attention to Pekrov and glared at him to keep him from coming unhinged. She then decided that she wanted a sandwich. Red had eaten the remainder of the AGB, so she had sulked for the last four hours. Now she was hungry.

She glanced at Red. His lips were white from how hard he'd clamped his jaw shut.

Lindy soured on the two parties. That brought the extra person into play. Rivka hadn't questioned his presence, but there wasn't supposed to be anyone else in the negotiations.

Rivka held up her hand and stood. "Who are you, and what are you doing here?"

"Zagreb. Helping Pekrov." He held his ground directly behind the labor negotiator.

"You look military. Are you a bodyguard?" Rivka took a step toward him, and he stiffened. "Call me Rivka." She held out her hand.

He lifted his, showing his palms. He had no intention of shaking her hand. Sometimes it wasn't as easy as others. "You'll need to leave," Rivka told him.

"I need to watch over Mr. Pekrov."

"You don't. Red, remove him."

Red slung his rifle and stepped forward.

The man crouched and assumed a hand-to-hand fighting pose.

Red grinned. "And I thought today was going to bore the snot out of me. Come on, fucker. Let's see what you got."

"*STOP!*" Rivka put herself between Zagreb and Ankh by stepping back. She didn't want the ambassadors to get caught in the violence. "What do you think you're going to accomplish by starting a physical altercation in here? Get the fuck out of here." She pointed at the air-curtained entryway.

Zagreb straightened.

Red maintained his stance. He wanted to fight the man.

"You are, of course, correct." He rested his hand on Pekrov's shoulder and gripped it harder than a friendly gesture would call for. "I'll be right outside."

Zagreb picked up his mask and prepared to put it on. He looked at Red. "It would have been my pleasure sending you to the emergency room. I expect that soon we'll get our chance to finish this."

"You will regret that day if you survive it," Red replied, backing out of arm's reach.

Zagreb tipped his chin and left the tent.

"He's a soldier," Red stated.

"Why did you bring a soldier?" Rivka asked Pekrov.

"I wasn't given a choice. He notified me that Elbird had taken sick and that I was to take his place. That's all I know. Are we not allowed deputies? For the record, I didn't know he was a soldier. I still don't know that for sure."

"These conditions are tightly controlled, and I'm sorry that I didn't call him on it sooner. We should not have started with an unauthorized attendee present. We shall file him as a suspected soldier. That does not look good for the labor side. Why do you have the army represented here when they are a government entity?"

"I don't care who they bring," Galwyn said, "but concur that we have to play by the same rules."

Rivka wanted to correct him, but he wasn't wrong. She returned to her seat. "Can you check with your military to identify that man? We do not need him to return. His superiors can deal with him."

"Rabble rouser?" Galwyn ventured. "Instigator? Yes. That is a good point. Please send me a picture of him, and we will run it through our database. Our military is not large, not more than five hundred soldiers, but alas, I have no interaction with them. My focus is entirely on the corporate effort."

Rivka looked at the SIs, who nodded as one. She almost laughed, but the situation was grim. She had forgotten something.

"I need you both to confirm that you will not light the sky on fire to teach the other a lesson. We cannot have you using the environment for leverage."

Galwyn leaned back and closed his eyes. "I'm not sure we can agree to that. The labor force may leave us with no choice."

"The environment is what it's all about," Pekrov told Rivka. "It is not only at the forefront of the negotiations, it is the lynchpin. Without it, the feds will not be able to hold it over our heads."

Rivka rubbed her temples. "You're both threatening to destroy the planet to teach the other a lesson. Do you understand how moronic that sounds?"

"I don't intend to sit here and be insulted, especially from one of your stature who comes so highly regarded. Your language is appalling. I shall report you to my superiors."

Galwyn shrugged on a light jacket, took a long time to adjust his mask as if waiting for someone to stop him, and then, without a final look back, he strolled out.

Rivka gestured at the entry. "Make sure Zagreb doesn't interfere with him."

Red pulled his mask over his face and hurried after the fed.

Pekrov and Rivka stared at each other. "I guess that'll be

all for today. Same time tomorrow?" Her smile was less than genuine.

"I guess," he replied. "Do you know if it was like this in previous sessions? I was led to believe that no progress had been made. That appears to be correct since we're starting over. Correct me if I'm wrong, although I don't think you have a problem with that."

Rivka chuckled. "Thank you for understanding. We remain at Square One. Let me ask a personal favor. Please find out about Elbird. I am concerned that all is not as it seems."

"I shall inquire about his health." Pekrov bowed and walked away.

"I think that went pretty well, don't you?" Rivka asked. She looked at Ankh for an answer.

Erasmus spoke using Ankh's voice. "I see that it wasn't our team that was at fault. They are dealing with sociopaths. We'll retire to the ship. If you need any Singularity representatives, please let us know." Ankh put on his mask and left.

Chrys, Billi Jane, and Tex followed him out.

Chaz and Dennicron made to leave, but Rivka stopped them. "Where are you going?"

Dennicron pointed at the door. "I thought we were all leaving. Aren't we?"

"Not yet. What did you see?"

Chaz raised his hand, nearly poking Dennicron in the face. "Sorry. My proximity sensors aren't operational." He turned his head with a jerky motion toward the Magistrate. His face covering was still in place in all its faux leather glory. "I saw that the two parties have nearly insurmountable personal issues."

Red returned. "Zagreb acted like he wanted to play rough, but staring down Blazer's barrel convinced him otherwise. Galwyn is clear."

Rivka nodded in approval. "Dennicron?"

"Chaz is correct."

Rivka looked at Lindy.

Lindy answered, "That bodyguard wasn't a bodyguard at all. He was the handler to watch Pekrov. They're gearing up to fight. He has no interest in negotiating anything."

Rivka tapped her nose. "The other players are of no consequence at this point except that they fulfill their roles as mutually antagonistic."

"What did you see from them?" Red wondered.

"Hatred, no middle ground. Their position is the only one. The feds don't care about labor, and labor hates the feds. Civil war is what they both seem to want. What they don't know is that it's the last thing they want. Anyone on this planet when they light up the sky will die no matter how righteous they consider their position."

"Can you make them see that? Maybe we should leave." Red pointed at the air curtain with his thumb.

"I don't know what it'll take to make them see the reasoning behind not destroying their planet. Their hatred prevents them from embracing common sense. Then again, the fed negotiator is looking forward to a weekend getaway with his mistress." Rivka scowled.

"I wondered what that was about. I should have known," Red admitted.

Chaz tried to nod, and his chin hit his chest. His head vibrated as the servos kept pushing his head down.

Dennicron hammered her fist into the back of his neck.

Chaz's head popped up. "Thank you!" He tried to smile, but only part of his lip rose. "This is most disagreeable."

Rivka watched the SCAMP's machinations. "Are you okay?"

"I'm really not, but my mind is sharp as a tic tac toe."

Rivka looked to Red, who bit his lip to keep from laughing.

"Maybe we better leave. Dennicron, do something with him until we can get him back to Rorke's Drift."

"I'm not leaving this case," Chaz declared.

Rivka studied his inelegant stance and hitched movements before she talked to Dennicron. "See what you can do to help his mobility and movements. I know it's harder in the ship than it would have been on Rorke's Drift. If necessary, take *Destiny's Vengeance* back there and get him fixed up properly."

"What if we switch bodies?" Chaz suggested. "Tex and I can change. Then Tex can go to Rorke's Drift, and I'll stay here."

"Is Tex good with that?" Rivka was skeptical. She shook her head. "What if we stuff you in with Clevarious again, and your body goes on a walkabout all by itself?"

"Not Clevarious! He's not good at sharing," Chaz whined.

"And you're not good at moving around. You're a wreck, Chaz. I thought they'd fix you better than this, even if only temporarily."

"They couldn't interrupt the production process, so they didn't do much besides rebuild my skull structure. Most of the time needed was to get into the production line when there was an opening."

"You mean Mildred blew me off?" Rivka leaned close to make sure she heard the answer.

Dennicron interjected. "You put it more harshly than it is. The factory is not geared for repairs, although they realized that repairs would be a necessary function, so Mildred is adding a repair section to the facility. It's not yet functional."

"They didn't do anything?"

"They rebuilt his skull and made this really cool Phantom of the Opera mask for him!" Dennicron nearly carried Chaz. Rivka put on her mask before they left the tent.

"Chaz, I hate to say it, but you better make peace with Clevarious."

"Can't I use my old portable device? Dennicron can carry me around her neck, placed delicately between her ample bosoms."

Rivka replied, "If you can get in there without losing any of yourself. You've expanded your consciousness since the old days when all you did was run my ship."

"I was titanically hugely gigantically enormously immensely gargantuan at that time, too. I'm more refined now. Like Red, strong but lean."

"Fine." Rivka didn't mean it was fine. She was done discussing it. She had misjudged what the plant was doing because she had assumed without getting particulars. Neither Ankh nor Erasmus had bothered to enlighten her.

Then again, she *had* slept for nearly twelve hours before meeting with Mildred and shortening the repair timeline. She wanted her team together, but that wasn't going to be possible. Chaz was a hindrance since he would fall over if anything happened. They could put him in the amulet and let him ride around with Dennicron while his body moved into the construction queue for a standard repair, which sounded like a new build, not a rebuild.

"Dennicron, work with Erasmus and the Singularity to get Chaz's body fixed. Chaz, into the necklace with your magnificence."

Rivka headed out. Red stayed in front of her by half a step. Dennicron walked with Chaz and Sahved while Lindy encouraged them to keep up.

"Do you think that smug bastard Zagreb will be back?" Red wondered.

"I think we won't see him," Rivka replied. "But he'll be close. We'll need the ship to maintain an infrared picture surrounding the tent because we need to know who's hovering nearby." Rivka switched to her comm chip. *Clodagh, make sure we maintain an IR and UV view of the arbitration tent and surrounding area. I want to know when people are nearby and watching.*

Already on it, Magistrate. We have one hundred percent coverage. It's nice when we get to park this close to the mission location.

Case. Case location. Don't tell me there are betting lines on this. It's an arbitration!

There was a long pause. Rivka had made it halfway back to the ship before Clodagh answered. *Okay, I won't tell you.*

"Ankh has a lot to answer for," Rivka muttered.

"You're not bent out of shape about the betting lines? We get one every case except that last one, where we were undercover. You know the deal, Magistrate. It helps the rest of the Federation embrace the rule of law in a healthy way while supporting the children."

Rivka stopped suddenly. Sahved bumped into her and mumbled an apology before stepping back.

"It's not for the *children.* It's gambling! A Federation-wide raffle on my foibles and my cases."

"First blood, first swearing. That second line already closed. Not your best effort, Magistrate, but close. It only took seven minutes and five seconds. First time we run, first punch, first arrest, and others as Ankh sees fit, and finally, case closed. This case was short notice, but many of the lines are still open for betting. We're already at a hundred thousand credits total value, which means fifty grand into the kitty."

"Kitty for the perfect case. No swearing. No punching. No blood and no running. Wouldn't that be nice, not to have to run or get shot or cut up?" Rivka mused. She'd been close once, but then the floodgates of Hell had broken loose.

"It's like you don't know yourself. Of course people are going to shoot at us. You're coming for their freedom, and bad guys don't take that well."

Rivka started walking, keeping her hands behind her back and her head down. "How far will Zagreb go?" she asked herself.

Red shrugged. "We'll be there to stomp his ass into last week if he crosses the line."

"Sometimes people need to have their ass stomped. I want to know more about him and Pekrov, as well as find out what happened to Elbird. Sahved, this is already more than an arbitration. I need you to look into Elbird. Coordinate with local law enforcement and check it out."

CHAPTER FIVE

<u>Tempran Silver, *Wyatt Earp*</u>

"Would you stop fighting the transfer?" Dennicron snarled.

Rivka leaned against the table in the engineering section of her ship. It had been turned into Ankh's workshop, then turned into the Embassy of the Singularity after SI Erasmus was made its ambassador. Ankh was a technical genius. Along with Ted—all hail Ted!—they had invented some of the key technologies employed by the Federation. The miniaturized Etheric power supply. One could run a heavy frigate like *Wyatt Earp*, but there were three on board because Ankh did research and development for R2D2, the R&D branch of the Federation.

Rivka tolerated the intrusion even though they tended to lock her out of Engineering on her own ship when Ankh was angry with her.

"It's like the question of how many Earths can fit inside Uranus," Red whispered. "One more if you just relax." He roared at his joke.

Rivka elbowed him.

"He's incorrigible," Lindy said, giving her husband the side eye.

Dennicron continued yelling at Chaz. "Archive those subroutines. You don't need anything related to running servos or maintaining facial expressions. I'll look exasperated enough for both of us."

That's funny, Chaz replied. *Hang on. Let me do it.*

"I can get a crowbar," Red offered.

Lights flashed on the device.

"Who left this place a mess?" Chaz said, using the amulet's speaker.

"You were the last one in there, Chaz, weren't you?" Rivka said.

"I don't know. You've had me slaving away on lawyer stuff after we called in the Bad Company and nearly broke the law and ruined your case. But besides that, I don't know."

"Thank you for bringing up that painful memory," Rivka replied. "Get that body back to Rorke's Drift. We'll pick it up on our way out of here unless you want to leave *Destiny's Vengeance* there and fly him back when he's ready. I'm not sure how long we'll be here."

Neither Ankh nor Erasmus answered. Rivka would have to get their approval to take their ship, energy-tethered to *Wyatt Earp.* Rivka liked having the second ship available at any time as long as Ankh or Erasmus was available.

Red waved and walked away, calling for Lindy as he went. "I see some serious gym time unless I can get some serious Pod-doc time. Magistrate?"

She checked the time. "Pod-doc is approved. A single time. Lindy, you drive that hoverbus."

"Hang on," Red countered.

Lindy waved at him by waggling her fingers. "You heard the boss. It's up to me how big I grow your ears, among other things."

"I think I should like that, but I have reservations."

They disappeared through the hatch.

Rivka turned back to Ankh, who was inside his hologrid.

"Do you know if they're coming out anytime soon?" she asked.

"The ambassadors are embroiled in Singularity business. It will probably be a while," Dennicron replied.

"That amazes me. Every time I'm in there with them, only milliseconds pass, but it seems like hours."

"Tells you how complex the subject is. It's an all-hands meeting of the Singularity to discuss the arbitration panels, along with the factory output. There are about a thousand other topics on the agenda, too."

"Why aren't you attending?" Rivka wondered.

"We are." Dennicron looked confused.

Rivka chuckled. She often forgot about their ability to multitask. They were capable of far more than any human until they were beaten to pieces. But Chaz survived what would have killed any warm-blooded creature. Rivka strolled out, leaving the embassy and their citizens to take care of business.

She found herself wandering the corridor, no destination in mind. The heavy frigate was a big ship, but it was not the ground. She could have gone outside to stretch her legs, but she liked the comfort of being home. She had no other home besides *Wyatt Earp*. Tyler still maintained quarters on Federation Station 7. She wondered why. Her resistance to marriage had nothing to do with a lack of commitment.

Rivka was happy with the status quo. Would anything change? That was what she feared the most.

She loved her team. It had finally settled. Red and Lindy. Chaz and Dennicron. Clodagh and Cole. Sahved. The pilots and their smuggled-aboard boyfriends. Ankh, Erasmus, and Chrysanthemum. And of course, Tyler Toofakre, DDS.

Good people all. It was the family she'd never had. She didn't want any of them to leave, although she'd already lost two crewmembers. Groenwyn and Lauton had become ambassadors on the faerie planet. It was a glory assignment, but not for someone like her.

She couldn't stand the peace and quiet. Neither could Red, who held the title as the only person ever to get ejected from the planet and given the nickname "Bristle Hound."

The faeries had interceded in Red's and Lindy's procreation. Their son Der'ayd'nil was part faerie, part Red, and part Lindy. He had wings and had grown faster than any human child. At less than a year old, he was the size of a six-year-old boy and flew around the ship.

After he was born, the faeries had imbued him with all the knowledge of their people. He spoke telepathically in mysticisms and riddles the crew didn't immediately understand. Since he was part faerie, he was an empath, too. He helped the crew over many of the hurdles that came with doing the job they did. It was emotionally challenging since they had to deal with the worst criminals in the galaxy.

This was the family that Rivka had chosen over the one she'd grown up with. She'd do anything for them.

Except give them time off, it appeared. She laughed silently. Some things were out of her control. They were the most important things, but that which was in her control inured to the benefit of her people. Like AGB deliveries, thanks to Ankh. They loved All Guns Blazing's menu, and the deliveries made up for any shortcomings the crew suffered when it came to creature comforts.

Rivka heard the flutter of wings and the scrape of claws on the deck and stepped aside to let Floyd and Dery pass. They were always chasing each other. Maybe that was why Floyd was losing weight.

Floyd flailed through the corner and bounced off the bulkhead before slipping and scrabbling toward Engineering. Dery cornered adroitly but slowed when he saw Rivka.

"Hi, little man," she said warmly. He flew into her arms, nearly knocking her over before tucking his wings. "One of these days, we're not going to catch you."

Dery laughed and shook his head. *You will,* he told her.

"You're right. Of course we'll catch you. What's up?"

The pain of success.

Rivka hugged him to her. "As usual, I have no idea what you're talking about. I'm sure it will be clear in due time."

Clear. Yes.

Rivka shrugged. She'd embraced her lack of understanding his insights. She would figure it out. Until then, she wouldn't worry about it. She couldn't because his insights were nebulous at the best of times. Always correct but often misleading. He wasn't even a year old, but he was already in tune with the universe, a state none of the others would ever realize.

They were okay with that. No one was trying to be anyone else. Of all the people she'd met in her life, the group surrounding her was the most comfortable with themselves. Even Rivka was settling into her skin and her role as a purveyor of life and death. It was the job, measured, assessed, and delivered.

Dery unfolded his wings, and they beat the air. He moved away from Rivka, turned, and headed down the corridor to where Floyd waited for him.

The wombat squealed and ran for Engineering, but Clevarious didn't let her in. She raced back toward Rivka.

The Magistrate stepped aside, and the two passed. She winked at Dery. He could have caught the wombat but lagged just far enough behind to keep her running.

"You're doing a service for us all," Rivka called before he rounded the corner. She ambled to the bridge, where she found one of the pilots and a Bad Company warrior.

Rivka tipped her chin to him in the way the warriors generally greeted each other. "Ryleigh, good to see you on the job."

The young pilot held her hands in the air. "Nothing to do while we're stuck on the ground but watch Clevarious watch the systems."

"Seems redundant." The captain's chair beckoned. It was comfortable, and she could roll her files across the main screen. "There's nothing else for you to do?"

"There's only so much sex one can have, Magistrate. Well, two, that is." Ryleigh adopted her best innocent look.

"I didn't know you and your aberrant sisters from different misters had reached that point. Go on. I'll watch the watcher for a while. Clevarious will call you back when it's time."

"Any chance for more AGB?" the warrior named Lewis asked.

Rivka stared at him without blinking until he stuffed his hands into his pockets and shuffled away.

"Magistrate!" Ryleigh said, jamming her fists against her hips and making herself big by puffing out her chest.

"What?" Rivka shrugged and threw her hands in the air. "Lewis," she said over her shoulder, "we will have more AGB, and we'll deduct the amount you and your buddies eat from your paychecks."

"Really? That seems kind of harsh. We ate for free on *War Axe*."

"No. I'm kidding. We usually have it at the end of a case. In the middle, too, if the case is annoying."

Lewis brightened and Ryleigh shook her head, smiling at the Magistrate.

"Is this case annoying?" he asked hopefully.

"It's shaping up to be that way. Now go on, both of you. I have some thinking to do."

The two hurried out and secured the hatch behind them.

"C, bring up this case file."

"Red told me to correct you to say 'mission' whenever you say 'case,' but I'm not going to do it because I know who the boss is," Clevarious replied, bringing the file to the screen.

"I'm pleased to hear that. I wondered what subterfuge Red has been up to lately. We should probably take him to Azfelius so they can put him in his place. If he wasn't trying to mess with me, I would think he was unhappy. I'm glad you recognize me as the boss, but I'd like you to think of me as a demanding friend."

"Ambassador Erasmus," Clevarious clarified. "He said not to antagonize you except when he approves it in advance."

Rivka looked at the ceiling as she always did when the SIs spoke since that was where their voices came from. "Erasmus approves the practical jokes that you play on me?"

"In advance." Clevarious sounded pleased with himself, embracing the timeline of engagements.

"How about no?"

"We can't have that," Clevarious replied. "You are held in the highest regard, Magistrate. We joke with each other to demonstrate our affection. Red made sure we knew that."

"He did, huh?" Rivka snort-laughed. "What about Tyler?"

"Man Candy is in on it, too."

Rivka closed her eyes. "His name is Tyler."

"I find that I'm unable to say that name. My programming has become corrupted."

"*Something* is corrupted. Fix your shit, C. Let me review this case a bit more. I have to find a way to leverage these two parties so neither one of them blows up the planet. Have Dennicron and Chaz join me."

A gentle knock sounded on the hatch.

"That was quick. Come on in. The party's in here," she yelled.

Sahved opened the hatch and straddled the frame, half on the bridge, half in the corridor. "Permission to go into town that I may so very righteously meet with the local constabulary for their critically important guidance and information regarding the members of the labor team who are missing in addition to the military who may have gone rogue."

"Sahved, you can tell me you're going. Hey, Magistrate, you're looking radiant! I'll be heading out to the local constabulary. Be back soon. Bye! Miss you already."

"If you're going, may I come with you?"

Rivka pointed. "No. I was demonstrating what you can say to me, and then you get on with your business."

"No, I can't come?" Sahved started to twirl the fingers on both hands, not as he did when he was happy but because he was stressed. He blinked rapidly.

"Let me rephrase. Yes, Sahved, you may meet with the law enforcement officials. Take Dennicron, Chaz, and Lindy with you." Rivka nodded solemnly.

Sahved brightened. "Thank you!" He hurried away without closing the hatch.

Tyler strolled in. "What's he so happy about?"

"He's learned that he can do the job I told him to do."

Tyler stopped. "That doesn't make any sense."

"None at all." She pointed at the main screen. "Are you going to do a free dental clinic while you're here?"

"Damn! We came here so quickly, I didn't think to ask." He studied the case file on the screen. "What am I supposed to be looking at?"

"The outdoors. That was my universal wave as opposed to my point of order declaration." She demonstrated a waving point and then a stabbing point. "See?"

"Not at all. I'll take your word for it." He looked up. "Clevarious, can you get out the word? I'll set up in the cargo bay. We can use the gravitic shield to keep the toxic air out. It'll be a pleasant respite for them to relax in clean air."

He hurried away without waiting for the SI's confirmation.

A piercing yap echoed down the corridor. Tiny Man Titan, a dog-like creature they had rescued from a forbidden planet. Some might say they'd kidnapped the dog, but he had gotten aboard, and they'd had to leave. Returning the animal hadn't been possible, so Clodagh adopted the creature and treated him like a king. The little animal spent most of his time curled up on her lap while she sat in the captain's seat.

The yapping ended with a shriek of pain.

Rivka was up and out the hatch like a shot. She made it ten steps down the corridor to find Clodagh cradling the dog while the big orange cat sat on the deck, cleaning his face.

Ankh made his way out of the galley and stood over the cat.

"You're mean!" Clodagh shook an accusing finger at the big orange.

"The dog's barking hurts his ears. Please teach it not to

bark, and it won't get the claw unless it does something else Wenceslaus doesn't like. Then it will." Ankh brushed past Rivka and walked down the corridor.

Tyler stuck his head out the door to the quarters he shared with Rivka. "Everyone okay?"

"Blood." Clodagh pointed at Titan's head.

Tyler examined the small creature. "He's fine. It's four little pinpricks. I assume it was him." He nodded at the cat.

Clodagh frowned. She carried Titan past Wenceslaus on her way to the bridge. The dog growled, making the chief engineer hasten her steps.

Floyd stumbled out of Rivka's quarters, fur matted from sleeping even though minutes earlier, she'd been running and playing.

Dery flew in from the cargo bay. He looked both ways, saw the corridor filled with people, and returned to the cargo bay.

Rivka watched her crew do what they always did.

"Business as usual?" Tyler asked.

"It could be worse," Rivka replied. "What if it wasn't business as usual?"

"Then we'd be in a world of hurt." He leaned against the doorway, cocked a foot up, and crossed his arms. "What's your next move?"

"I need to find some way to counter each of these groups' arguments. We're treating it as a mediation, but I think we need to make it an arbitration where the two parties are not in the same room at the same time. We've called it shuttle diplomacy. I'll have to go back and forth, but if we can keep them from blowing up this planet, we'll declare victory."

"They both want to blow up the planet?" Tyler shook his head. "At least if they wait, the locals can go out with good teeth in their heads."

"That's morbid, but I like it. We can't blow up the planet today, sorry. Your uncle's roommate's cousin's friend's sister has a dental appointment."

CHAPTER SIX

<u>Tempran Silver, Capital City</u>

"What I wouldn't give to not be here," Lindy mumbled, staying alert.

Sahved was in a life-and-death verbal struggle with the chief of the local law enforcement.

Chief Brindlemar was having none of Sahved's arguments regarding his concerns about Negotiator Elbird's health and well-being.

"I am so very impressed by your magnanimity and graciousness in hosting the Magistrate and her team on your wonderful planet…"

"I already said no. Plastering your lips on my ass isn't going to change my mind."

The law enforcement office had a utilitarian flare, with four desks and no separate spaces for officers or interrogations. Crime wasn't a big concern in Capital City. People generally kept to themselves and stayed indoors. The limited visibility implied a criminal's paradise, but it wasn't. The people were there because they were miners or supported the mine. Government employees lived in a different area of the city, walled off from the rest.

"If I may," Dennicron leaned close, "we're going to produce a search warrant in support of the conflict resolution between the government corporation and the labor force." A second later, Dennicron added, "The warrant is in your inbox. Please check it, and then we'll be on our way. If you come with us, it'll ensure that all goes in accordance with your laws. Otherwise, we'll follow Federation procedures, which are a little more open than Tempran law."

"Which means if I don't go and you shoot up the place," he looked pointedly at Lindy's railgun, "I'll be to blame."

"At least that's what the people will see." Dennicron nodded.

The chief scowled. "Why don't you let us handle it?"

"Can't. Federation was called in to prevent civil war. You don't want that. We will do everything we can to keep the parties from coming to blows."

"Maybe. Labor is being unreasonable. Feds are bending over backwards to accommodate them."

Dennicron didn't take the bait. Neither did Sahved. The two sides were entrenched in their positions, and neither was willing to give credit to the other.

"We need to check on Mister Elbird if you'd be so kind."

The chief grumped back to his desk, then searched the computer, wrote an address on a piece of paper, and grabbed his mask. The others followed him out. Only Lindy slipped the full-face breathing system over her head. The chief looked at Sahved and Dennicron. "Suit yourself."

Outside, they found their vehicle waiting. The trip to

the far side of town took longer than it should have since they couldn't drive very fast.

Limited visibility plagued them the whole way, but they'd expected that.

It would have been quicker to fly, but it wouldn't have been as illustrative. Living as the locals lived in the atmosphere and seeing the city from their viewpoint helped Sahved and the others to understand and ingrain the problems they faced.

"How long has the atmosphere been this bad?"

"As long as I've been alive. It may be worse nowadays, but who knows? I could never see my neighbors down the street. We didn't always have to wear masks, though. With a stiff breeze, we could enjoy the outdoors for a spell."

"Where does the fresh air come from?"

"Outside the city, away from the mines. There are vacation spots an eight-hour drive away that are mask-free zones."

"But there's no ore in those locations."

"The reason the city exists is because of the air. To consider the air a plague is denying the reality of our existence. Yes, masking up sucks, but it's always been that way. Blaming the government and threatening to blow us up because of it is asinine."

Sahved was hunched over, but he had twisted his head to look Chief Brindlemar in the eye. He found he had nothing to say. Learning both sides of the problem was instrumental in finding the middle ground.

He couldn't wait to talk to the Magistrate. The blank look on Dennicron's face suggested she was researching the chief's claims to determine their veracity. As he'd learned from the Magistrate, the truth came in a great variety of shapes and sizes, each person embracing their own version of it.

"This is Elbird's apartment. If he's taken ill, I would suggest keeping your masks on." Only Lindy wore one. "Mask, singular. I don't understand how your physiology can metabolize this stuff."

"You haven't been to Yemilore, a ring planet. Our sky is the other side of our world. We're made a little differently," Sahved replied ambiguously.

They left the vehicle and headed up the stairs in the direction the chief pointed. He referred to his printout to make sure they were in the right place. When they reached a door that looked like a dozen others, the chief knocked. When he didn't receive an answer, he knocked a second time, then shrugged.

"We'll enter the premises under the Federation warrant issued by Magistrate Rivka Anoa," Dennicron announced. The amulet around her neck flashed a green light. Chaz agreed.

She bumped the door, and it popped open. She didn't need to take a run at it or do anything more than leverage her weight and robotic strength.

"Hey!" the chief said. "You didn't have to break it. We could have gotten the manager."

"Next time, speak up a little quicker," Chaz suggested.

"Who was that?" The chief looked from face to face.

"Chaz. He's right here. There are two of us." Dennicron pointed at the device that held Chaz.

"Pleased to meet you, Chief. Let's get to work! The door is open, so to speak."

"Wait." Sahved blocked the entryway. "There's been a struggle. See how to the left, we have disturbed items on the shelves, but to the right, everything is neat."

"That's what you see?" The chief looked at the Yemilorian in disbelief. "I see a messy guy who was trying to clean up his act and stopped halfway through."

"I have to agree with Sahved," Chaz said, and Dennicron nodded.

"I'll wait outside. You clearly have your agenda, which I do not. For that reason, maybe I'll stay to make sure the government isn't railroaded by a rogue Magistrate." The chief glared through his mask.

"Truth isn't an agenda," Lindy said from behind the group. "It is what it is, nothing more and nothing less. It is the foundation of a decent society. Would you deny us the right to investigate within the limitations that brought the Magistrate to Tempran Silver? There are considerable stakes here. You stand to lose as much as anyone. Not just your job but your life and the lives of your family. Please let these seasoned investigators do their job."

Sahved raised an eyebrow, then bowed to Lindy and went inside. "What do you see?" he asked Dennicron.

She used the sensor suite built into the SCAMP, which included infrared, ultraviolet, and millimeter wave. She pointed at one area. "Blood splatters."

"Don't even need UV to see them," Sahved said and took a knee to study the floor. "Is it fresh?"

"It's completely dried, but with an air purifier running, it could be old. This evidence is inconclusive," Dennicron declared.

"I concur." Sahved stood and moved carefully around

the apartment, avoiding touching anything even though his fingerprints looked nothing like a human's.

"I've informed the Magistrate," Dennicron announced.

"You can do that? How?" the chief wondered.

Dennicron wanted to ignore the question, but she decided to take a lesson from Rivka in not creating an enemy where none was needed. "We have comm chips integrated into our bodies that we can use to communicate privately with everyone on the team. All of us, Lindy and Sahved included. We're not that far from the ship, so there's enough range."

They finished their inspection and found nothing besides the blood splatters, which wasn't enough to make a determination that someone had been killed in that apartment.

"We still need to find Elbird, and we're no closer to that," Sahved said. "Next stop, labor's offices."

"You can't go there during the arbitration," the chief stated categorically. "You *cannot*."

"I assure you, we can," Chaz said from the amulet.

Tempran Silver, Capital City, Government-Corporate Offices

With the possible foul play regarding Elbird's disappearance and Rivka's decision to engage in shuttle diplomacy, they'd taken the ship to the government offices.

Red adjusted his mask, grumbling the whole time.

"Suck it up. It's so you can breathe, that's all. Nothing really important."

I go, Dery told them.

Rivka and Red both frowned. "I'm not sure that's a good idea. We don't have a mask that will fit you."

Dery shook his head and smiled.

"He can use mine," Red said. He took off his mask and wrapped it around Dery's head. It didn't provide a tight seal, so Red increased the airflow to blow a constant stream of fresh air into Dery's face. "My nanocytes will take care of me."

"I'm sure they will. We can share if need be." She lifted Dery's chin. "Why do you want to go, little sweetheart?"

He smiled behind the faceplate of his mask.

Rivka hadn't expected an answer, and she didn't get one. "We shouldn't be outside long."

She stepped into the airlock with Red and Dery, and it cycled.

Red coughed with the addition of the tainted air. He covered his mouth and straightened. "It's nothing. Like swallowing a pinecone."

Rivka fought not to laugh. When the outer hatch opened, Red stepped through, squinting to limit how much air got into his eyes. They watered as if he were having a hard cry, but that kept the orange soup from damaging his corneas. Although the nanos would repair any damage, Red could be temporarily blinded. He couldn't do his job if he couldn't see.

Dery fluttered between Red and Rivka.

We're on standby, Cole told her. *The whole squad is suited up and ready to go.*

The combat suits turned the warriors into mechs, complete with rockets, oversized railguns, and armor that protected the wearer. It gave *Wyatt Earp* and the Magistrate significant combat capability, and then there were the experimental weapons Ankh and Erasmus installed on occasion. *Wyatt Earp* currently sported an ion cannon rivaling the best on any Federation ship, along with a cloak and shields. There were lasers, too. Those were old-school but highly effective.

Rivka was both blessed and cursed. Her rulings made her a target of the Federation's major criminals, including many with their own small fleets of warships. She could project power as needed and call in the Bad Company if the situation took a turn for the worse. The Bad Company, a private conflict resolution organization, was led by Terry Henry Walton and his werewolf wife Charumati. Rivka had made it possible for the Bad Company to collect a three hundred and fifty million credit reward for the recovery of priceless art.

Terry Henry would drop everything to help Rivka.

She walked across the small courtyard. *Wyatt Earp* took up most of the empty space. Red held the door, and she walked in. Dery flew through the opening and waited. Red reached under his son's wing and patted his back.

"You make a good father," Rivka noted.

"I do my best, but I'll be damned if I can teach him the joys of the stand-up pee."

"I wouldn't know," Rivka said, quickly looking away. "Let's see where we can find Galwyn."

She stopped the first person she saw and asked, but they looked at her like she had two heads. They hurried away when they saw Red tapping one finger on his railgun.

"Do you have to do that?"

"Lightweights need to know their places. They're afraid for no reason."

"Doesn't mean they're not afraid."

Red smiled. "I'm teaching them it's stupid to be afraid for no reason."

"I don't think that's the lesson they're taking away from your brief meetings." She nodded at a group of individuals coming toward them, two uniformed security guards and one bureaucrat. Rivka walked toward them, holding her hands up.

"You can't be in here!" the one that Rivka instantly nicknamed loudmouth shouted.

Rivka pulled her credentials from the pocket of her Magistrate's jacket and held them in front of her. "I assure you he can. I rate personal security under Federation Laws, Appendix D, Chapter Seven, Section 1, Armed Security for Heads of State, which applies to the Federation's judicial representatives called Magistrates. That's me. Where's Galwyn?"

"He can't be in here with that," the guard repeated softly.

"Knowing the law and applying it to each situation is a critical skill that each law enforcement professional should embrace."

"But..."

Rivka cut him off by shaking her finger at him. "Don't say it again because you're wrong. He *can* be in here with the weapon he's used on multiple occasions to protect me. Seems like criminals don't like being held to account."

"I can see how you make people angry," the bureaucrat said without introducing himself. "Magistrate, you'll find

Galwyn this way. I'll escort you if you don't mind. All of you."

The guards flanked Red and Dery. Rivka walked beside the bureaucrat.

"What do you think about labor's position?"

"It's idiotic," he replied. "We can't move the mines because we can't move the veins. They're morons for embracing an ideal that doesn't exist. The city exists because of the ore. Without the ore, there is no city."

"You could move the town. Temp duty for mining operations, but you don't have to live on top of the mines. Not anymore."

"But we've always lived here," the bureaucrat replied. "It's like asking us to become Blokites."

"No one is asking you to become a Blokite. I've met exactly one of them, and it was a most unpleasant experience. Flexing to the situation isn't surrendering. It's adjusting to reality."

"You don't know anything about Tempran Silver. We're not the kind of people you can order about."

"No. You're the kind of people who would torch the atmosphere to keep the other guy from benefitting. It would be a Pyrrhic victory at best."

"Whatever." He motioned at a closed office door.

Rivka thanked him and waved him away. She had gotten all she needed from him. She avoided touching him because she didn't want to see into his mind. She was certain he'd been truthful with her.

The two security guards followed them to the office. Rivka knocked twice before entering. Red made sure Dery went through. He looked at the guards and shut the door in their faces.

"You're different," Galwyn said. He scowled, then his face changed. His expression turned to one of shame. "I'm sorry. That was uncalled for. Welcome to my office. What can I do for you?"

Galwyn stood and gestured at the two chairs in front of his desk. Rivka sat, and Dery settled against her. Red stood with his back to the door.

"I'm going to talk with each side in this disagreement individually. That is at the heart of arbitration: remove the friction within a room populated by people who are antagonistic toward each other. I want to find where your boundaries are when I suspect you and the labor group probably mostly agreed. There has to be a compromise where you are both dissatisfied, but it forestalls a conflict. The Federation cannot have a civil war on any of its planets."

"Exactly!" Galwyn ejaculated. "Bolarium six is a critical mineral for the Federation and the Singularity in particular. It is found on Tempran Silver and one other planet, but the other planet is even more hostile than here, and the cost of mining is three times as much."

"That doesn't mean the mines have to run at all costs," Rivka replied.

"I think your assessment of where we agree with labor is overly optimistic, to say the least. They don't want to mine at all, so we don't agree on anything."

"They're willing to mine, just not here," Rivka countered. "Why don't you allow people to live far away from here? Provide aerial transport. Eventually, a town will take shape, and then it'll become a city. And you can keep mining."

"Sounds good from an outsider's perspective. If you lived here, you'd know that wouldn't work."

"How would I know that?" Rivka asked.

"You'd just know. The only livable place is currently a resort. There isn't enough room for a city. It would destroy the ambiance and ruin the air."

"The air is ruined because of the mine." Rivka was running out of patience, and she'd only just begun. "Your mistress will forgive you if you can't take her there."

"I doubt that. I don't know how you found out about her, but so be it. I'm a man with needs, Magistrate."

Rivka leaned away from the desk to make sure none of Galwyn's errant emotions or thoughts bled into her mind.

"The most important thing is that you find a place to bend your demands into something the labor team can agree to."

"Oh, no, Magistrate. We are not going to surrender our superior negotiating position just so you can add another feather to your cap and carve another notch on your man's railgun. Not at our expense. We hold all the cards. Don't let them terrorize these negotiations. They can't threaten to torch the sky. We won't have any of that."

"Isn't that what you threatened to do?"

"Only if we have to."

"Now you sound like *you're* crazy." Rivka looked at Dery.

Fear, he told her.

Rivka nodded. "What are you afraid of, Galwyn?"

"Afraid? I'm not afraid of anything, least of all Elbird

and his band of misfits." Galwyn crossed his arms in a classic defensive pose. He was afraid of *something*.

Rivka stood and walked around his desk. "Bullshit." She punched one hand into the other.

Red stepped into the middle of the office.

"What are you afraid of?" She grabbed his arm and looked into his mind.

Losing his job and the perquisites that came with it. He was finally in a position that he had dreamed of. He was somebody. He didn't want to go back to being a nobody. Labor would ruin that for him. Galwyn pulled away before Rivka could see more.

"What was that? What did you do to me?"

"I did nothing to you, Galwyn. Your position is a little selfish, don't you think?"

"I worked my whole life to get here. I'm not going to give it up just because of some malcontents. We'll get rid of them, and the rest will see reason. No one is blowing up this planet. If we have to, we'll send in the military and secure those who would do us harm."

"By sending in the military, aren't you the ones who would be doing harm?" Rivka countered.

"Not at all. We don't want to do it. They're making us do it."

"Said every abuser in the history of humanity." Rivka returned to her seat but didn't sit. She picked up Dery. "We'll be leaving, but understand that I know where you're coming from. When I rule on this case, you'll have to live with it. Right now, you're not looking to be on the right side of history, and I order you not to take military action against labor or anyone else on this planet. Violation of that order will earn you a trip to Jhiordaan. That'll put a big crimp in your plans. Your side chick will have to find someone new."

His lip lifted in a snarl. Rivka twirled her finger. It was time to go.

CHAPTER SEVEN

<u>Tempran Silver, Capital City, Labor Office</u>

"Where is Mr. Elbird?" Sahved demanded.

Zagreb stood to the side of the desk at which Pekrov sat with his arms crossed. He feigned a yawn, not bothering to cover his mouth, and looked at Zagreb.

The soldier replied, "He's already told you he's home sick."

"He is not," Sahved stated. "Where is he?"

"How are we supposed to know what a grown man does when he's supposed to be home sick? Maybe the stress of the negotiations was too great."

"What do you mean by that?" Dennicron pressed, closing with the men.

"Stress is the number one cause of most health issues in men. You should know that. You're a robot," Zagreb taunted.

"Not a robot," Dennicron replied flatly. "What did you do?"

Zagreb recoiled as if he had been punched and flung his

hands up. "Whatever are you implying?"

Pekrov called for calm as he assumed the role of peacemaker. They knew he wasn't aware of what happened to Elbird since the Magistrate had looked into his mind. Zagreb had stayed away from her. He was the mystery.

The chief had not yet shared what they'd found out about Zagreb and his military service. Was he still on active duty? If he was, they could recall him and remove him from influencing the labor team.

Sahved made a decision. "I'm sorry, Mister Zagreb, but you'll have to come with us for questioning. We need to know more, starting with why you're here."

Pekrov stood and gestured for Zagreb to stand behind him. "You will not take anyone from my team while the arbitration is happening. That is one of the precepts in coming to the table. Me and my people are exempt from arrest during the talks. It's in the guidelines of the arbitration."

Sahved looked at Dennicron. Her eyes blanked as she reviewed the information and contacted the ship to talk to Rivka. When she returned to the moment, she had the answer. "My apologies. We will not be taking Zagreb for further questioning, but we *will* continue our investigation into the disappearance of the person who was leading this arbitration. His disappearance is highly suspect.

"We believe that something bad has happened to him. If you won't be forthcoming, then we'll be inclined to think it was you. We'll respect your immunity at this time, but these negotiations will come to an end when the Magistrate makes her determination. Then we'll get to the truth." Dennicron nodded at the door.

Sahved bowed his head to Pekrov. "We'll talk again," he promised.

The group departed, leaving Pekrov and Zagreb behind.

"Do you know where Elbird is?" Pekrov asked.

Zagreb held a finger over his lips and waved for Pekrov to follow. They went next door and took the elevator into a basement, then followed a corridor to steps and descended one more level.

"They probably put a listening device in your office. It's no longer secure until we gut the place. I'll have my people take care of it," Zagreb explained.

"You're scaring me," Pekrov said. "If you had nothing to do with Elbird, why would we take care with our words?"

"You don't need to worry about what happened to Elbird. Focus on the negotiations. When the Magistrate shows up, you're going to tell her that we want control of mining management. We're not going to work for the government corporation anymore."

"But that's not our position," Pekrov countered. He tried to ease away from the soldier, but Zagreb stayed toe-to-toe with him.

"It is now. It's what compromise is all about. Elbird didn't want to push for control. He wanted the feds to take care of it. That's not optimal. We want control, and the price of bolarium six needs to double so we maintain our market share while more than doubling our profit. That needs to come into labor's coffers, not the feds'."

"So you did have something to do with Elbird's disappearance. Did you kill him?"

"I told you not to worry about that." Zagreb draped his

arm over Pekrov's shoulder. "Stay focused on the Magistrate. She'll see the validity of your argument, especially when you concede about staying co-located with the mines. All the action that makes Tempran Silver what it is happens in Capitol City. The feds will get their cut, but that's it. They don't need to be running the show. We'll even buy air purifiers for the home of every miner. It'll be the least we can do once the new profits start rolling in. Don't you think it's better if we take care of our own?"

"Of course we want to take care of our own. We can do that through a strong contract." Pekrov tried to sound brave and committed, but Zagreb was larger and stronger. The look on the soldier's face bordered on maniacal. Pekrov was cornered. "What if I can get the feds to give us what we want without demanding we take overall control?"

"I don't see how that'll work. You'll have to explain it like I'm a small child."

Pekrov wasn't sure what he could do to sway the intransigent government nor how to convince Zagreb. "Elbird was better at this than I—"

Zagreb interrupted him. "He wasn't very good at this at all. Get yourself under control. You're going to win a huge victory for labor. Embrace that."

Pekrov didn't bother mentioning that the victory seemed to be in Zagreb's best interests too. If the feds gave up management of the mines, who would step into that lucrative void? He was sure Zagreb had a new team ready to go.

But first, Pekrov had to convince Zagreb that it could be done without overthrowing the government.

He smiled and held out his hand. "We all have our battles to fight if we are to get through this thing called life. What would it take to get air scrubbers for the whole city? That would clean up the planet. Double the price and use the extra for atmosphere generators. The technology is there. They use it to turn uninhabitable planets into wonderlands."

"That takes decades," Zagreb argued.

"When's the best time to plant a tree?" Pekrov asked. "Twenty years ago, but the second best time is today."

Zagreb shook his hand. "Don't screw this up with pie-in-the-sky crap. This is all or nothing. If the Magistrate rules against us, we're as good as dead. You better play your role well, or we'll find someone else who can."

Pekrov held his hand in front of Zagreb until the man took it, and they shook. "I'll give you my best, and if that doesn't get us to a better place, I'll step down and leave this planet for good. I hear the slavers are hiring drudges. I can drudge."

Zagreb smirked. "I can get behind someone who's such a nut. You're on. Get us what we want, or sell yourself into a life of drudgery."

"It's like a shrubbery but completely different." Pekrov joked, but his thoughts did not reflect the mirth that showed on his face. His mind raced to find a way out, but he kept returning to the issue at hand. He needed to deliver a win during the arbitration. That was the only way for him to survive.

"We better get back. I'm sure the Magistrate will be calling shortly to meet with you. She has already met with

Galwyn, and it seems she gave him the business. She may be more receptive to what you offer."

"How do you know she met with Galwyn or what they talked about?"

Zagreb cupped Pekrov's cheek with his hand. "It's Tactics 101. Know what the enemy is going to do and make sure you're there first."

"Doesn't answer my question."

"There are some secrets that need to be kept, Pekrov. Respect mine, and I'll respect yours."

"I don't have any secrets," Pekrov countered. "I'm a nobody."

"We'll see," Zagreb replied mysteriously.

Wyatt Earp settled into the field behind the labor offices. That land had been reclaimed from a mine that had run its course. Nothing grew since the dirt used to fill the pit had come from the mine, minus the topsoil, which had been sent to government-managed farms. Without the topsoil, there would never be any growth besides straggly weeds.

At least it provided a firm base for the heavy frigate.

The vehicle carrying the rest of the team rounded the building and stopped near the extending ramp.

Red rolled out, wearing the mask he'd liberated from Dery. He wanted to make sure Lindy was okay.

He could have used his comm chip, but that was the last thing he thought of. His was a hands-on personality.

The group stepped out of the vehicle, along with Chief Brindlemar.

Have him join us on the ship, please, Rivka requested. *Tell him we'll have tea or something.*

"The Magistrate has invited you to see her ship. There will be tea, I'm told," Dennicron said.

The chief nodded. Dennicron led the way and Lindy followed, making sure no one was left behind. Sahved lumbered along, lost in his thoughts.

Watch your head, Lindy told him.

He jerked back into the moment and ducked. He held up two fingers in a peace sign.

They had to transit the airlock in groups, but Red made sure it went as quickly as possible. He and Lindy entered last. The chief and Rivka were in the corridor by themselves. Red went on alert despite Rivka's relaxed body language.

"Chief, thank you for going with my team while we work to learn what happened to the negotiator from the labor team. I look forward to hearing their debrief." She smiled to disarm him.

"It is my hope that we find him quickly to allay any fears you may have regarding subterfuge."

"Do I have such fears?" Rivka asked. "Come." She took his arm and guided him down the corridor. She called over her shoulder. "Red, rally the team in the conference room."

He kissed Lindy and made to go, but she grabbed his arm. "I'm going, too."

Red grunted. "I knew that."

Dery joined them as they walked down the corridor. "Clevarious, call the team to the conference room, please," Red requested.

"Already taken care of," Clevarious replied. Footsteps

echoed down the corridor from both directions.

Dennicron hurried toward them from Engineering. Sahved walked behind the Magistrate.

"The gang's all here," Red whispered. He side-hugged Lindy.

Dery projected positive thoughts and feelings to them. No words, but they knew it was him. He flew between them and threw his legs forward so he could sit cockeyed on their shoulders. He wrapped one small hand around Red's neck and the other around Lindy's, hanging on as they walked.

The chief glanced at them, leaning around Sahved to see what there was to see. "What is the small creature?"

Rivka laughed. "Dery is Red's and Lindy's son. He was conceived on Azfelius, which means the faeries had their hands in things."

"That's very strange," the chief said. "The boy has wings and flies?"

"He has all the knowledge of the faeries, and he's less than a year old."

"'Faeries?' I've never heard of that race."

"They keep to themselves," Rivka replied. "It serves them well."

Sahved held the door, and people filed into the conference room.

Rivka took her seat and had the chief sit next to her. The others took seats around them, except for Red and Lindy, who stood by the door.

Rivka began. "What can we do to secure the proceedings? I don't want to see any more changes in the personnel."

"If there are changes, then there are. We can't make anyone stay on one side or the other." The chief smiled.

Rivka stared at him. "You need to be more proactive about encouraging them to stay the course because if we want a positive resolution, it will require the same people working through concessions until such time as we can declare an agreement that both sides hate but one they can live with."

"It's a strange way you have, Magistrate. If you know that both sides will hate an agreement, then why would you force it on them?"

Rivka chuckled. "All good compromises consist of agreement where no one gets exactly what they want. If they got what they wanted, it would mean one side capitulated. Surrendered. That's not a compromise. I've been at this for a while, despite how young I look. Arbitration is about finding the best option for both sides, whether they hate it or simply dislike it."

"I'm not sure that's going to work here. We have specific needs that must be taken care of. The miners mine. The government makes sure the product is sold, among other things."

Rivka nodded. She didn't want to verbalize anything to the chief that he could misconstrue as her taking one position over another.

"The miners mine," Rivka started, "but they aren't mining right now. How do you think that makes them feel?"

"Why should I care how that makes them feel?"

"Crime, Chief Brindlemar. Crime usually follows a loss of work or a significant change in status. There's a logical progression to the depths people will descend to when their fortunes have gone sour."

"Crime is not an issue in Capitol City."

"Then why do you have a force of four officers?"

"There's crime, of course. More admin code violations than anything else, but we handle it so it doesn't become an issue. We take care of what needs to be taken care of."

"What do you do if there's a kidnapping or a murder or another violent crime?"

"We don't have such things, but we have a manual to guide us if the worst came to be."

Rivka couldn't believe they didn't have the crimes that defined most civilized societies, especially with conditions so dire. Then again, maybe people stayed indoors and away from each other *because* the conditions were so bad. Without social interaction, there would be no reason for violent crime. Then again, the worst crimes were perpetrated by friends or lovers.

"You don't have domestic violence? The people are forced to stay inside together. Too often, that doesn't end well."

"We are a calmer people than what you're used to. We don't have such things. People attack their partners? How does that work?" The chief gasped the words as if they were being wrung from his body.

"It works at a visceral level and is all too common throughout the Federation. Tempran Silver would be a rarity without such crimes. It would be a pleasant surprise."

"Would be? I just told you we don't have those crimes. It is fact."

"Thank you, Chief. I'm used to caveating everything. I am a barrister before anything else, so please don't take it personally." Rivka stood. "I think we're finished here. I need to talk with the labor team. I already had a conversation with Galwyn and will probably return there later this afternoon. Shuttle diplomacy means an inordinate amount of back-and-forth, but I am confident it will be worth it and the effort will *not* be in vain."

The chief offered his hand, and Rivka took it.

"Domestic violence is a thing," she muttered.

His thoughts went to the instances of familial violence. The numbers were significant, but all they did was move one party out of the home. Children went with their mothers, always. It was the way of things on Tempran Silver. The chief wasn't sure that was right.

"There is hope for Tempran Silver," Rivka stated. "Red, if you could escort our guest out, I'd appreciate it."

Even at Red's smaller size, he loomed over the chief. Brindlemar walked briskly down the corridor.

"What did you see?" Sahved asked.

"That domestic violence is common, but they sweep it under the rug. I knew it. You can't lock people up together and expect roses, wine, and moonstokle pie. Well, maybe you *can* expect that, but you're not going to get it."

"Common definitions of terms, Magistrate. It sounds like they have all the things they denied."

"A rose by any other name, Sahved. That's why I wanted to see his thoughts on the issue. Get with Dennicron and dig into Tempran law. Find me the terminology I need to use for them to understand. They are embracing a reality that I don't see."

"On it!" Sahved bounced up. He nearly cracked his head on the ceiling but caught himself in time. He rushed into the corridor and ran toward the bridge. He stopped when he realized Dennicron was going the other way and turned around to join her in her quarters.

"Sahved," Rivka called softly. "What's going on?"

The Yemilorian hung his head lower than usual. "I feel like I'm not contributing to the team. Maybe I'm not trying hard enough. I shall try the hardest you would ever see a person try, wearing out the deck plates with my running to achieve—"

Rivka stopped him by holding up her hand. She smiled. "Sahved, I think you're trying too hard. Slow down and walk at a measured pace. It's not the hare that wins the race but the tortoise with his slow and steady approach. Walk with confidence, Sahved. Decide what needs to be done and then do it."

"This job is better than I deserve. I was First Assistant to the Special Deputy Undersecretary to the Secretary for Health and Well-Being to the Minister of Internal Security. It sounds impressive but was a nobody-doing-nothing job. Now I have real responsibilities, nebulous as smoke drifting on a raging wind."

"You've been reading historical fiction again, haven't you? You're right that your duties are nebulous, but they are centered on stopping crime and making the planets we visit safe places for people to live and work. We deal with the worst of the worst, so it may seem skewed regarding how many good people are around. They are the unseen faces we work for."

"I thought we worked for Grainger and the Federation."

"Grainger is a prism through which the light shines. We work for them." She pointed at the bulkhead to indicate the world outside the ship. "Everywhere we go, that's who we work for."

"What if the labor team turns out to be bad?"

"Then we'll find that out, and we'll remove them so the rest of the workers can benefit from new leaders who are honest and law-abiding. We'll make sure the government corporation doesn't take advantage. Our job is important. We do what needs to be done, which creates powerful enemies. But we will still do it. If we don't, what happens to them?" She pointed in a different direction.

"I understand. Slow is smooth. Smooth is fast. Wyatt Earp was a smart gunslinger."

"Marshal. Yes. We named the ship after someone who put his life on the line for Justice every single day." Rivka clapped his arm.

"I shall endeavor not to work harder than possibly necessary to tentatively achieve a meritoriously joyous result, maybe," Sahved replied before his stomach started heaving.

Rivka stepped back. "It's been a while since you got airsick, but we're not even flying."

"I feel it. There is movement. Oh, my." Sahved dropped to his knees and spewed a green mass that didn't look like anything the team had recently eaten.

"Are you sure it's not related to breathing that nasty air?" Rivka asked. "Clevarious, summon the cleaning bots. They have some work to do."

"The ship is moving, Magistrate," Clevarious

confirmed. "A seismic event is centered only three kilometers from here."

"An earthquake or something else?"

"Ship's sensors are ill-suited to this task, Magistrate," Clevarious replied. "I am scanning local communications for more information."

Rivka rubbed her chin before deciding she still had work to do. She headed for the airlock, stopped, ran back to the conference room, grabbed her mask, and returned to the task of meeting with the labor team.

Red waited for her at the airlock. "I hate this thing." He waved his mask while Dery giggled.

"Me too, but you're wearing it. Sahved just puked. I think it was the air."

"Not the earthquake?" Red did a dance called the shake and bake.

"I didn't feel it. There's no way that made him sick. He's gotten over his air sickness, so it had to be something else. The only thing that was different? The air. Deductive reasoning on display. Put it on, and let's go."

They masked up and stood in the airlock while it cycled the good air out and the orange air in. After the outer hatch cycled, they left for the labor office. Red walked beside Rivka with Blazer at the ready. Even with the mask on, he scanned the area for any threats to the Magistrate.

The ground rolled, quick and jerky. Rivka and Red braced themselves for the ten seconds it continued. The tremors stopped as quickly as they'd started.

"What the hell?" Rivka wondered. "I don't think that was an earthquake." She took off running for the door to the labor building.

CHAPTER EIGHT

<u>Tempran Silver, Capital City, Labor Office</u>

Rivka and Red entered the offices. The foyer was set up like an airlock. They passed through after a rough air exchange and walked into the building. People were running around in panic.

"What happened?" Rivka asked, but no one stopped to answer her question. She continued to the labor leader's office. Elbird's office was clearly labeled, even though he was no longer in there.

Illness. Rivka didn't buy it, but she had to play the hand she had been dealt while Sahved investigated the disappearance. Let her team do what they needed to do so she could focus on delivering this planet from the hell the two parties threatened. She seemed to be the only one in the negotiations who didn't want to blow up the planet.

A gaggle of workers waited outside the office. Rivka bumped to the front of the line. "Hey!" one of the miners complained.

Rivka held up her credentials but then backed down. "What's got everyone so spun up?"

"A cave-in, lady. In our business, that's what we call bad. They pulled us out of the mine before we had the roof properly shored up. It came down, and then the next section did a little while later."

Rivka sympathized with the men. "Did anyone get hurt?"

"No one was in the mine. We're on strike, aren't we?" he countered.

"Then why is everyone freaking out?"

"It changes the stability in the mine, and worse, it changes the surface dynamic. The earthquake following suggests there's more damage than what we know about. The entire system could be ruined. The amount of work we'll need to get back to where we were is mind-boggling. If we started today, there might be no bolarium six for months."

"You've lost your negotiating advantage," Rivka suggested.

The miner shrugged. "I don't care about that. We have to get into the mine and start fixing it."

"But you're on strike." Rivka gripped the man's arm. She wanted more insight than he was sharing verbally.

"It's our mine. I spent my entire adult life down there."

Rivka saw his love of his trade. He took ownership of the mine. His anger grew at the circumstances that prevented him from being underground, one with the rock.

From surface mines to underground, the miners worked with the ground and not against it. It wasn't through force of will but a shared goal: remove only the minerals the planet wasn't using.

Rivka let go of his arm. "I'm sorry. I want to resolve this quickly so you can get back to work."

He grunted in agreement.

The door opened, and frustrated miners exited. The next group wanted to go in to tell Pekrov the same thing the others had.

They were putting pressure on the leadership to resolve the strike. They'd been set back. Since they were paid for the amount of bolarium six they delivered and not hours of work, their incentive to hold out for more pay and better conditions had disappeared. They were looking at months without pay.

Pekrov called for order. "We've heard your grievances. Trust us that we'll work in everyone's best interests. We won't be seeing anyone else today."

Rivka waved her fingers at him. "I think you'll see me."

He looked like he didn't want to, but common sense prevailed. He ushered her and Red inside and secured the door behind them. He flopped down behind his desk and pulled a bottle and two glasses from his drawer.

"A guilty pleasure, Magistrate. Today has turned ugly. We're not going to bow to pressure from our members. They know not what they demand. They'll have to trust that I'm working in their best interests."

Rivka took the proffered glass, which held a caramel-colored liquid. One sniff told her what it was. Whisky.

"Single malt?" she asked.

"You understand. I took you for a blasphemous cretin. I may have been mistaken. Sometimes, surprises are good."

Rivka held up her glass in a toast. They clinked, and each drank. Rivka drained her glass. "I'm here to ask what you have to have from these negotiations, and don't give me any optimum state bullshit. You know that won't work. The government needs to see a concession. Maybe we can start with what you *don't* need. Give me something, Pekrov."

A door behind the negotiator opened, and Zagreb stepped in. He shot Rivka an icy glare before his eyes settled on Red. His lips thinned as he pressed them together, then the corners of his mouth twitched up.

"No." Rivka stood to block Zagreb's view.

He refocused on her. "No, what, Magistrate? I should say no as well. You shouldn't be discussing the arbitration without me present."

Rivka stuffed her hands into her pockets rather than give him the finger and turn Red loose to beat the man senseless. She took comfort in the familiar grip of Reaper, her neutron pulse weapon. She could put him out of her misery. Rivka knew he would be a problem, but despite that, she couldn't just kill him. That wasn't how the law worked. She'd have to wait for him to cross the line.

"You aren't the negotiator. My conversation is with Elbird, but since he conveniently disappeared, Mr. Pekrov is next. You're nobody to me or these conversations."

"You have your security. I'm his." He jerked his chin at the labor negotiator.

"Red, wait outside, please." She tapped her pocket, and Red nodded.

He left the room.

"Your turn. Get the fuck out." Rivka dialed her neutron

pulse weapon to one, the lightest setting. It would cause him a great deal of discomfort.

He had bluffed, and she'd called him on it.

"I'll be right outside if you need anything." He gripped Pekrov's shoulder until his fingers turned white, then left through the rear door.

Rivka was sure he was listening at the door, if not using a device tapped into the room.

"You'll have to forgive my friend. He is very protective of the union and its people."

Rivka waited to see if he would answer her previous question, but he didn't.

"What are you willing to concede, Mr. Pekrov?"

The office started to shake slowly at first. Then the gyrations picked up the pace. The tremor lasted for a full minute. Rivka continued standing to ride out the waves.

Pekrov closed his eyes and groaned with the shaking. "That's the worst thing that could happen to us. Earthquakes, cave-ins, and destruction of the underground mines. This is the end of us."

"You can't fight Mother Nature. She will always win. Maybe your air will clear up."

"This isn't funny. Without the mines, we are nothing but a bunch of people on welfare looking for our next handout. That's not us. We're miners!"

Rivka was happy to see his energy. Maybe there was hope. "What if this exposes new veins?"

The door burst open, and a man dressed in miner's coveralls ran in. "We've lost Gildar!"

Rivka waited for the distraught man to say his piece.

"Gildar." Pekrov put his head in his hands and rocked.

Rivka asked, "What's Gildar?"

"The newest shaft and horizontal runs. Three hundred meters deep. A dozen levels covering a hundred square kilometers. It's the biggest of all our underground mines, and it was the most productive." The man dropped into the seat Rivka had occupied and lamented his existence in a series of whining moans.

A commotion outside the open door signaled something that had nothing to do with the loss of Gildar. The sound of flesh violently contacting flesh was unmistakable. Rivka ran out to find Zagreb holding his face, on which there was a clear handprint.

Red stood on the balls of his feet, angled to offer a minimal target to his opponent.

"You fucking weasel dick!" Zagreb shouted.

Red smiled. He'd slapped the man across the face, the ultimate put-down for someone who considered himself Red's equal.

"Come on. I'll put you on your ass, and we can call it a day. I've had about enough of you."

"Who hit first?" Rivka asked.

Red pointed at Zagreb. "He rabbit-punched me in the kidney. I guess he doesn't understand what body armor does."

"I was getting your attention. It was like a tap on the shoulder," the soldier argued.

"Then why didn't you tap me on the shoulder?" Red asked.

Rivka bit her lip to keep from laughing. *Touché, Red.*

Zagreb looked about but didn't find what he wanted—a weapon. Red waited patiently.

"That's enough. Red, back in the office. And you." She pointed at Zagreb. "Stay out. That's enough of your physical threats. I'll not have it. One more, and you'll find yourself in my brig."

Zagreb smoothed his clothes. "I daresay you wouldn't like the fallout from such a precipitous action, Rivka. You would pay dearly if you attempted to arrest me."

"Red, kill him with your railgun. We don't have time for his antics."

Red took a step back and looked at Zagreb and Rivka. She nodded at the soldier. "Finish him. He's a problem, and my job is to remove problems."

"I can take him," Red said.

"Shoot. Him. With. Your. Railgun." Rivka enunciated each word.

Red pulled Blazer from where it was slung over his shoulder.

When Rivka got the look she wanted, she held up one hand. "Wait."

Zagreb and Red both looked at her.

"That's how easy it will be, Mr. Zagreb, if you continue trying to fuck with me. I will have you removed, not just from our proceedings but from life. Stay the hell away from Mr. Pekrov, and stay the hell away from me and any of my team. Do you understand me?"

"You can't give that order, and I won't follow it."

"At your own risk. You've been warned." Rivka knew she didn't have a legal footing to remove him if Pekrov wanted him in attendance, but she could bluster. If he attended, she had the authority to muzzle him. "Red." Rivka gestured at the office, and they entered.

They found Pekrov refilling his glass.

"Another?" he asked the Magistrate as an afterthought. With her nanocytes, she couldn't get drunk since they would neutralize the alcohol when it reached her bloodstream.

"Why not?" she replied, knowing misery loved company. By drinking his whisky, he would have less available, and maybe they could find shared ground. "At least no one was in the mine."

"At the very least," Pekrov replied. He saluted with his glass and took a long drink.

"Sabotage?" Rivka asked.

"What?"

"Did someone decide the negotiations weren't going as they should and it was time to start the war?"

"We can torch the sky, but no one messes with the mines. No one. Neither side of this dispute benefits from the loss of the mine. No, Magistrate. I think this was a result of the cave-in. It triggered an instability that progressed through the strata. We would have been fine had we been able to shore up our work before the stand-down. And that wasn't the last of them, I suspect, but it will be the last of the earthquakes that hurts us." He drained his glass and poured another.

"What do you really want, Mr. Pekrov? What is the one thing you must have, without which you'll go to war and destroy the planet?"

"That's the hardest question you'll ask. There are many things we need to have, but if I were to ask for a catchall, it would be decent conditions for us to work and live. That's not too much to ask, is it Magistrate?" Pekrov was slurring his words.

Rivka held out her glass for Pekrov to top it off. His hand shook so badly that she stopped him and took the bottle to pour her own drink. She capped it and moved it out of arm's reach.

"It's not too much to ask for decent conditions. I'll see what I can do." Rivka looked at her glass and decided not to drink it. She left it on his desk and stood. "I'm off to meet with Galwyn and see what his must-have is. I'll be back."

Red preceded Rivka out the door. She left the door open and kept glancing back until she saw what she expected–Zagreb entering the office through the back door. She made sure he saw her watching him before she left.

Outside, Red turned on her. "What do you mean, kill him? That was fucked up."

"Before this is over, we're going to have it out with him and whoever his group is. If they are soldiers trying to foment unrest, they're doing a good job of it. I think they killed Elbird, but I can't prove it, and he won't let me touch him."

"I can hold him down for you, but next time, let me beat him into next week. I'll pummel him so hard his grandkids will have bruises."

"I guess I closed the swearing line," Rivka added.

"You did that at the first meeting in the tent. It was like you had a smart missile with an F-bomb attached already launched, and all it needed was a target."

"At least there's no blood, and how about we keep it

that way?" Rivka raised her eyebrows at her bodyguard and friend.

"Did you like that handprint on his face? Candy-ass tried to backstab me. It pains me to think he got behind me, but I was trying to watch the door, along with all the asswipes in a panic. It won't happen again."

Rivka nodded. "Talk about taking his masculinity down a notch or two. Then again, you've made an enemy for life, but I'm good with that. In this business, everyone we run into has the potential to be an enemy. Can't be helped. Criminals don't like being caught."

Clodagh, prepare the ship. We're headed across the city to see Galwyn.

CHAPTER NINE

<u>**Tempran Silver, Capital City, Government-Corporate Compound**</u>

Rivka stood outside the building. The main door was locked. Galwyn was in, but the work day had ended a half-hour prior. They hadn't been constrained by the mine collapse. For them, it was business as usual.

Did they understand the scope of the damage? If they weren't miners, that answer was probably no.

"Security is on their way, Magistrate," Red said.

Lindy, Sahved, and Dennicron, carrying Chaz, had joined her for this iteration of shuttle diplomacy.

"Ideas?" Rivka asked.

"We can use *Wyatt Earp* to look for a new vein of bolarium six. If we find something close to the surface, that would minimize the impact on both parties," Sahved suggested.

"Ask Clodagh to do that now. Take the ship over the collapse so I can see the extent of the damage while they're airborne. We'll call them when we're ready to go."

Rivka could have made the request, but she was trying to share the load with her team.

Cloak the ship. No sense in letting everyone see you. These people will make up something that sounds horrendously vile, like that we're doing the other side's evil bidding, Rivka added to the order to take the ship out. Her trust was limited to begin with, but after meeting with the parties, she knew it was best not to trust anyone or give them fodder to make accusations against her. She'd done enough by starting a personal war with Zagreb.

That guy rubbed her the wrong way. She knew he was the one behind the threats from labor. He could be driving toward civil war. Rivka doubted he would be willing to accept anything from the feds.

Pekrov showed more flexibility...until Zagreb got to him.

The soldier's last look before Rivka turned away suggested Pekrov would change his mind by their next meeting.

She'd deal with that when it happened, or if Pekrov suddenly became ill and another negotiator stepped in. She didn't want to think about that. It might stall the negotiations or precipitate action. The planet was at risk as long as the two parties remained at odds. The miners were losing their faith and confidence.

Irrational actions were imminent if they couldn't calm the masses. Then again, maybe they were already underway. Not in blowing up the sky but in removing the issue over which they fought—the mine.

"Too many conspiracy theories," Rivka counseled herself. "Just stick to the facts."

The night guard opened the door and ushered the group inside. "You know where you're going."

He walked away without a second look, but he scowled at the courtyard. "I thought you came in your ship. How did you get in here?"

"The ship dropped us off," Rivka replied. *Wyatt Earp* was doing the survey she had requested.

"Makes sense." He disappeared around a corner to continue his rounds.

"He's not concerned about Galwyn's health and safety," Red mused.

"He shouldn't be since if we wanted to hurt him, the only thing that would happen is the guard would get hurt, too. He probably has more common sense than the rest of them." She didn't bring up Zagreb since it would spin Red into the ceiling. She wanted to see Zagreb get what was coming to him, but not at the expense of the negotiations. Rivka wasn't going to play Zagreb's game, either. He had been warned that she was in charge.

Galwyn's door was open while he worked behind his desk. For once, he looked busy. Documents were strewn across his desk in the form of locally made plastisheets. Wood pulp was a rarity.

The lack of trees and greenery contributed to the planet's poor air filtration. Tempran Silver needed atmospheric generators. She would talk to the Federation about investing in one or more for the security of the bolarium six source.

If they retained it, Rivka noted, devolving into negative conspiracy theories.

"Good! You're here. I have a shuttle waiting so we can

visit the collapsed mine. I think those bastards did it to spite us!" He grew more upset with each word.

"Then let us take a look, Galwyn. Please, be patient about assigning blame. We just came from the labor office, and the loss of the underground is tearing their souls apart. They spent their lives' sweat digging in there. Its loss was a spear right through their hearts."

"So you say. I still think they did it!"

"No one did anything," Rivka argued. "I suspect it was a consequence of pulling out of the mine before they could shore up the roof in the new section. If they don't seal cracks with plasticrete, then they could expand and lose structural integrity. When one section fails, it affects the next section. The cascade failure was inevitable. The delay in these talks is what caused this if anything."

"I'm not to blame." Galwyn stood and gestured at the door.

"You probably are." Rivka smiled. "At least, that's how my report to the Federation will read."

"Why are you after me? You detest competent leadership, or is it my other work affairs that have you down? Not getting enough, Magistrate? Sorry, but my social calendar is full, although I could probably work you in if you begged me hard enough."

Red stepped forward. Rivka stopped him before he grabbed the government-corporate negotiator.

"Like I said, your fault. Now, let's take a look at that cascade failure."

He walked ahead, taking an obvious sidestep to get past Red without moving within arm's reach.

Red walked between Galwyn and Rivka to a shuttle waiting out back.

The shuttle's crew waited by the door. Galwyn introduced the group.

"Neat trick, Magistrate," the pilot said. "How your ship disappeared right after it took off. Is there any way you could share how you did that?"

Rivka looked at Dennicron. The SI didn't lie well. She could only imagine what Dennicron and Chaz would come up with, so she quickly replied, "We have a technomage on board. She coordinates with the universal Etheric to queeze the bobbaling."

The pilot nodded. "Keep your secrets, then."

"I think that's best." Rivka clapped him on the shoulder. He had been amused by the answer. He knew it was a new technology he had never seen and was suitably impressed.

"You have an invisible ship?" Galwyn asked.

"Not as far as you know," Rivka replied more sarcastically than she'd intended. She didn't like the man. Still, she was a professional, and she needed to stop her snark. "I'm sorry. Yes, we have a ship that can stay out of sight and out of mind."

"That's unacceptable. We need to know where your ship is at all times. To avoid any unintended miscues, of course."

"We'll ensure we don't fly into anything, Galwyn. Don't worry about where my ship is. Let's focus on those mines, shall we?"

The man scowled as they traveled the short way from the compound to the site of the destruction. From the surface, it didn't look alarming. The underground entrance was intact, with a crease traveling away from it into the distance.

"What am I looking at?" Rivka asked.

Galwyn shrugged.

Dennicron pointed. "Downward pressure. That V is pushing the rock down instead of being inverted, which relieves the pressure underneath. The geology of this area is unstable."

Dennicron had downloaded information about mining en route. It took her a second to learn what the miners spent years studying, but the first-hand view was enlightening.

Rivka turned to Galwyn. "What are you going to do about this?"

"Get the miners back to work. Probably turn this into an open pit mine. The tailings pile is going to get pretty big. Maybe we can build a ski mountain."

"Are you kidding?" Rivka realized he was, albeit in a sordid way. His only concern was getting the miners back to the mines.

He smiled. "Take us down," Galwyn told the pilot.

After they landed and exited the shuttle, they found the collapse to be more pronounced than it had appeared from above.

"This is as close as we should go," Dennicron advised. "My data suggests the collapse could expand."

"Nonsense," Galwyn said. "Go as close as you want."

The ground shuddered as if the land were scoffing at Galwyn's guidance.

Rivka shook her head. "You first."

"As you wish." He took one step and stopped. "I guess this is close enough."

Rivka looked at her team.

Lindy whispered loudly through her mask, "If Dery were here, he would be crying in sympathy with the planet's pain. It has to be in agony."

Rivka took Galwyn's arm and jerked him back. "You're responsible for this."

He ripped his arm away with a violence Rivka was unprepared for. "How am I responsible? And don't ever touch me again."

Red growled behind his mask, and the moisture from his breath briefly fogged the faceplate. His nostrils flared while he clenched and unclenched his fists. Rivka held up one hand to forestall him from taking action.

"You stopped their work before they were able to shore up the section they were expanding."

"That's nine levels deep. It shouldn't have affected this." He pointed in a direction Rivka didn't bother looking. "And it's that way a couple kilometers."

She understood that the first two quakes had been deep, and they had compromised more of the underground structure.

"This changes the negotiations," Rivka stated.

"It does. We all lose unless the miners get plugging. We'll have to move the surface equipment here. Haul trucks, loaders, scalers, all of it."

"I hate to say this, but the first thing we need to do is confirm no one was down there, and the second thing is that we have to meet with the labor side. First thing tomorrow morning. I'll inform them, too. You can leave. Take your shuttle." Rivka waved him away.

"What about you?" He shook his head. "Never mind. Your invisible ship will come for you, even though you have no comm equipment with you."

"Yes." Rivka waved once more, then crossed her arms, making no attempt to shake his hand.

Red stood close by, being his most intimidating. He had gone into the Pod-doc for an additional treatment and regained half his previous size. The debate about further treatments was ongoing.

"No one was in the mines, Magistrate," Galwyn called over his shoulder.

Dennicron summoned *Wyatt Earp*. The ship landed not far from the shuttle, which had not yet taken off. The outer hatch was on the opposite side, so Dennicron led them around. They entered and took off while the shuttle remained. To the pilot and Galwyn, it would have looked like Rivka and her team disappeared.

"What did you have in mind?" Dennicron asked. "I admit that I'm lost in regard to the negotiations. There doesn't appear to be a resolution."

"At the moment, it looks like nothing but dead ends. Tomorrow's meeting should give us a new foundation. In the meantime, I need to call Grainger."

Billi Jane and Tex met them after they were through the airlock. With blank expressions on their faces, they waited for news.

Rivka leaned close to them. "It wasn't you. Both these parties seem unwilling to compromise, and now with the mine collapse, things are a hundred times worse. I've helped nothing by being here."

Billi Jane activated her surprise subroutine. "I don't understand."

"Humans can be irrational. Sometimes it takes an even more irrational act to show them how to get back on track."

Tex nodded rapidly. "What do you have in mind?"

Rivka laughed since he was the second SI to ask that question in two minutes. "I have no idea," she replied since she didn't. She hoped one would come to her before the morning meeting.

CHAPTER TEN

Wyatt Earp, in Orbit over Tempran Silver

"No blood, no arrests, no punching. You're losing your touch." Grainger stared at Rivka through the screen.

"I hear the line on swearing has closed. That has to count for something."

"Not your fastest by far. Not your slowest, either." Grainger smacked his lips. "What did you want?"

She took a deep breath. "Both parties want to destroy the planet because both negotiating sides are unhinged."

"Business as usual, then."

"I want the Federation's commitment to deliver two atmospheric generators to Tempran Silver, along with the Bad Company in mechs. I know they showed an extraordinary ability to operate underground. We need to kickstart these negotiations, and that means I need to offer something, like reopening the mines without the miners having to do work they've already done once."

Grainger stopped making faces. "We can't do any of that."

Rivka stared at him, and he stared back. "Then you set me up to fail, High Chancellor. Moving this needle is going to take a titanic effort unless you're willing to write off Tempran Silver and the mineral they provide, bolarium six. I know this sounds like a trite argument, but when you have a single source for something, you do what it takes to keep that supply train rolling. I hope you'll be able to convince the powers that be to take action on this. I'm calling Terry Henry to see what he might be able to do."

"Good luck. The Bad Company is dealing with pirates who tried to invade Butternut Crinklefries or whatever that damned planet is called."

"You are a strange man. Stranger than the danger of Grainger."

Grainger rolled his eyes.

Rivka reinforced her point. "Atmospheric generators. Two."

Grainger nodded once and signed off.

"C, get me Terry Henry Walton."

Clevarious was quick. "*War Axe* is engaged at present. Are you willing to wait?"

"Engaged? Are they fighting someone?"

"Yes, they are fighting off space drones. Would you like annoyingly boring music while you wait?"

"Why would I want that?" Rivka scratched her head. "Are you okay, C?"

"I am fine. My research suggests this type of music makes people happy after their call is finally answered. The feeling of relief results in an overwhelmingly positive experience."

"Waiting to get your call answered results in a positive experience?"

"Not at all. It's the relief from being aurally tortured that is uplifting. You should try it sometime."

Rivka looked at where the annoying sound was coming from. She was upset until she realized she was being trolled. "Nice one, C. Now turn that bullshit off. I'm calmly in the moment, dropping some oms while enjoying life."

"What in the fuck are you doing?" Terry Henry sounded annoyed. "I blew up a ship just to take your call and find you waxing Buddhalistic. Don't be a nutbag, Rivka. What did you call me for, and don't say to assess my calm. I'm in the middle of a glorious ass-kicking, and the jury is still out on whether it's mine or theirs. Do you like that? 'Jury is out?'" He laughed uproariously.

"Can you provide a show of force over Tempran Silver so the parties in contention don't blow up the planet to prove the other wrong?"

"Shut down the party that wants to blow up the planet," Terry advised.

"They are threatening the same thing. Both of them. It's the most fucked-up thing I've ever seen," Rivka replied.

"Let them."

"That's what Red said." Rivka chuckled. "Of course you would both think the same way."

"Hang on." The image bounced. In the background, someone shouted that they were firing the mains. Terry growled an affirmative. "Gotta run. My people, your people, lunch, all that."

The screen went blank.

"Looks like we're on our own, C. Contact the parties

and let them know the negotiations resume tomorrow morning at the break of dawn. We're going to start early and stay for as long as it takes. We're going to resolve this tomorrow. Period."

Rivka stood, waved, and left the bridge. There was no one there to wave to, but she did it anyway. She couldn't trademark the move, but she strove to make it her own.

In the corridor, she found Tyler waiting. "Why didn't you join me?"

Tyler smirked. "Sounded like you were talking to Terry Henry. Those conversations are best when they aren't interrupted. He gets distracted as easily as you do."

"I'd say that hurts, but it's true. I have a lot on my mind, and it's easy to go one way over another."

Tyler nodded. "So, what did you get him to do for us?"

"Not a damn thing. He was fighting pirate drones. Sounded intense. He promised he'd call back, nothing more."

"Will he?" Tyler pressed.

"Probably not, since it wasn't really a promise. More of a quip inside a joke surrounded by sarcasm."

"Sounds like him. For what it's worth, that sounds like Red, too."

"What sounds like me?" Red asked from down the corridor.

He walked toward them with a towel wrapped around his neck. Lindy and Dery followed. Dery had a small towel draped over his head.

"Terry Henry suggested we let them destroy the atmosphere."

"Good. Can we go? This place sucks. Wearing a mask?

That's some serious bullshit."

"Hey!" Lindy glared, then smiled at her giggling son. "Don't say those words. They're not good."

I know. Dad is funny, the boy said in everyone's mind.

Rivka furrowed her brow and peered around Red. "No thought-provoking words that no one can understand?"

Dery continued to laugh.

Tyler nudged Rivka. "Thank you for your clarity. Your father is clearly a bad influence."

"He is," Lindy agreed.

"I'm not. Words flow like a river, carving the landscape to the path of least resistance lest the waterfall end."

"What?" Rivka wondered, pointing at Red with her right index finger and pointing at Dery with her left.

The flow cannot be stopped, but it can be redirected, Dery added.

Lindy beamed. "So, who's a bad influence on whom? I may have been mistaken, which I'm not going to say very often. Time to work out."

Red paused and waggled his eyebrows. "Or, we could hit the Pod-doc for one more treatment."

"No." Rivka waved them away. "Tomorrow morning at the crack of dawn, we'll be in the tent, ready to meet the negotiators. We'll need to bring snacks and coffee, and we'll stay there until it's resolved. That is tomorrow's plan. Commit to nothing else."

"Do I get to pummel that smug bastard into next week?"

Dery giggled.

"Once again, I find myself telling you no, but maybe one of these times, I'll say yes."

"Maybe, and I'll be here when you do!" Red smiled and pounded down the corridor. Lindy shook her head.

Beware the surrender to fate, Dery told them as he passed.

They watched the family disappear around the corner.

"What the fuck?" Rivka asked. "He couldn't stick with speaking clearly?"

"He's not even a year old." Tyler looked into Rivka's eyes to see if she understood his point.

"The child's voice is the one we can understand. The faeries' voices are different." Rivka stared at the bulkhead as she descended into deep thoughts. "Makes me think he's seen the planet die. We don't want that. I hope they make it to the morning so we can have a candid conversation about the future of Tempran Silver. If only these minerals were somewhere else."

"They are, but they're a lot harder to mine."

Rivka sighed. "Even if they torch the atmosphere, someone else will appear and begin the exploitation anew. Someone like Minerals Intergalactic. They'll be happy to gain a monopoly on bolarium six, especially if they don't have a population in the way. We need to protect the current population, which is exactly where we started. We need to protect them from themselves."

"Do you need me for this conversation?" Tyler quipped. "We have a cat who's probably hungry. A wombat, too."

Rivka surrendered to the inevitability of it all.

Morning came early, as Rivka intended. Days blended into nights, which blended into new days. Space lag was worse between worlds with different orbital days. The Yollin time constant standardized days and schedules between planets but nothing else, and definitely not a human's biorhythm.

Sometimes, Rivka slept for sixteen hours straight to catch up. Even with her nanocytes, her body needed rest. They all did. The quick transfer to Tempran Silver from Rorke's Drift had left them day-challenged and time-compressed.

At a different time and on a different planet, it would have been called jet lag, which was a pale version of what Rivka and her crew endured.

"Coffee, you shit-sucking blowhole. What the fuck is this, herbal tea? How about you eat a cauldron of dicks?" Red roared from the galley.

Rivka halted with her double-sized mocha. She slurped it to get his attention.

He glared at her, then pointed at the food processor on the bulkhead.

"Problem?"

"Can I use your processor to get a coffee? Ankh is fucking with me again."

"What if the crew is conspiring to keep you healthy by providing nourishing sustenance and not crap?"

Red stabbed a finger at Rivka's mocha. "I want coffee. And what if the crew is a bunch of nob-hobbled butt-hugging hair lips?"

"I think I should be more insulted than I feel," Rivka replied. "Food processor, please deliver a double-shot latte with chocolate and whipped cream on top, almond soy."

Red twisted in a circle. "Are you trying to poison me?"

"One ketchup smoothie, coming right up," Clevarious announced.

Red glared from one face to another, stopping when he got to Lindy since he knew better than to get mad at her. "It's a conspiracy. That has a legal definition with a precedent set in law by legal authority. A conspiracy! I'm going to sue."

"The fuck you are." Rivka waved as she walked away. She stopped and reviewed her wave. She lifted her hand over her shoulder and turned it back and forth rather than shaking it from side to side. "See you slackers at the airlock." She waved in her new style and continued into the corridor.

She heard Red cheer when the food processor delivered a cup of straight black coffee. She had coordinated with Clevarious to make sure Red got what he wanted. C hadn't thought it was Ankh who'd reprogrammed the food processor. He had more research to do since there were many programmers on board who could mess with the system so well that no one could find the intruder's tracks.

Rivka strolled slowly. According to her internal clock, she had twenty minutes before they needed to be in the negotiation tent. She wanted her team to be ready, and that meant Red and Lindy had to get their coffee.

Tex and Billi Jane waited in the corridor. Rivka nodded a greeting.

"We have the snacks," Tex said unnecessarily. They both carried trays covered with clear wrapping.

"You've not been relegated to being a drudge. Give me one of those trays, and I'll carry it." Rivka held out a hand, gesturing for Billi Jane to hand over her tray.

"Can't do it, Magistrate. You're still the boss."

"Then I give the orders, right?"

"Of course," Tex replied haltingly.

"Then follow my orders. Hand over the tray."

Billi Jane reluctantly complied.

"What is this?" Red bellowed.

"Easy, big guy. You're making a lot of noise for this early in the morning," Rivka said.

Lindy added, "That's what *I* told him."

"Quick brief. We're going to wait them out. I have a couple things I will offer. If I can get them to accept, then we'll have to convince the Federation to fulfill the promises. Like, two atmospheric generators."

"Won't that solve their problem?" Billi Jane asked. "We suggested it, but the Federation shut us down before we could put it on the table."

The Singularity had its own resources, but for something like an atmospheric generator, which was a planetary asset, no one person could redirect one from its current use. It would take the entire council. Could Rivka paint a picture of a compelling need to sway the majority of the ambassadors away from current use? She was counting on her persuasiveness as well as being willing to call in favors from as many ambassadors as needed.

Erasmus could also broker a deal or two with SI labor to gather the necessary votes. Would he be willing? Rivka couldn't say.

"We will see what we can do. I intend to keep them here until we reach an agreement. If we must, we'll move them to the ship to sleep and eat before we continue. I can't have them continuing their threats." The group nodded. Rivka's plan made sense, and neither of the two parties was. They would never agree at their current pace.

Rivka needed to speed things up before they spun out of control if they hadn't already. The mine collapse might have set the negotiations back, but Rivka believed there was still a way forward despite the geological concerns.

They put on their masks and left the ship. They found that during the night, *Wyatt Earp* had returned to where it had parked when it first arrived on Tempran Silver. It was a short walk to the tent, and to no one's surprise, they were the first ones there. They made sure the air scrubber was working before they removed their masks and set up the snacks and drinks.

Rivka sat in her initial position, with one chair across the table to her left and one to her right. She drummed her fingers on the table while she waited.

Sahved and Dennicron, carrying Chaz, arrived. Rivka nodded politely.

"I missed the wake-up call by a single second. The time it takes for a bullet to leave the barrel of an ancient blaster on its way to annihilate a target. This is the shattered soul I bear to you this morning for my complete and utter failure in time management. It could be the worst non-wake-up in the entire history of Yemilore. I should be flogged for my transgression. Flogged with real cats' tails!"

"Would you shut your soup-sucker?" Red said. "You're here before the negotiating parties, without which there's no party at all."

Rivka waved dismissively. "What Red said."

"I shall stand at the wall and watch the proceedings to learn the machinations of humanity in the throes of crisis."

Rivka shook her head. "Sahved, you are in rare form today. Let the parties talk. We'll compare notes later."

"I will be happy to share my notes, but I have to return to the ship. I left my datapad."

Rivka shook her head once more. "Me, too," she lied. It was in her jacket pocket. "We'll take mental notes for comparison."

Sahved radiated joy as he stepped back. From the tent wall, he eyed the pastries. He had skipped everything to join Rivka before the others arrived.

Good. That'll teach him to be on time, Rivka thought.

The crack of dawn came and went without anyone joining them.

C, did we get confirmation of the meeting time from each party? Rivka asked.

We did, Magistrate. They both knew the exact time.

Time passed. Thirty minutes became an hour before the tent flap rustled and Zagreb walked in. Rivka looked past him to see no one. He had come alone. He took the seat set aside for the labor representative.

"Let me guess. Mr. Pekrov has taken ill."

"It is a tragedy that such a debilitating illness has run rampant through the ranks of our most senior officials. So tragic."

"Lead poisoning?" Red blurted.

"I don't think so. We do not have lead deposits on Tempran Silver." Zagreb looked sideways at the big body-guard. "Am I missing something?"

"Bullets are often made of lead," Red explained.

"That is not an allegation you want to make, asswipe."

Red's smile faded.

Rivka stood. "Enough. We will continue with you, but understand that I'm going to send a team to look for Mr. Pekrov."

"I expected as much," Zagreb admitted. He leaned back and crossed his arms to assume a devil-may-care pose. He stared at Rivka.

She schemed about how she could touch him to interrogate him properly. He knew where the bodies were buried, and she wanted to discover his secrets.

"Sit down, Rivka. I'll not let you touch me. There are rumors you use it to read minds. Is that true?"

"Not sure where you would have heard such tripe, but that rumor is going around. Do you *actually* believe people can read minds by touching someone else?" She made herself sound skeptical. Interrogations were about acting. Gaining the confidence of the accused until they were comfortable enough to tell their story. Rivka should have assumed Zagreb was tied into the criminal network.

"I'll avoid any unpleasantness between us," Zagreb replied. He maintained his pose, glancing at Red and Rivka. If they tried to force him, he'd have to fight. The look in his eye suggested he preferred engaging with the Magistrate before Red.

Behind him, Lindy eased her railgun's barrel into position until it was pointed at him. She mimed pulling the trigger.

Red tipped his chin in her direction while not taking his eyes from the third labor representative in three days.

"Where's the feds? Does this mean that they've surrendered?" Zagreb asked.

He has a point, Rivka thought.

CHAPTER ELEVEN

<u>Tempran Silver, Negotiations Tent</u>

"Billi Jane and Tex, I'd like you to check on our wayward government corporate representative." Rivka gestured at the air curtain.

The two took the hint and hurried out.

Rivka and Zagreb sat in silence while the others stood by the inner wall. Rivka caught Sahved checking out the pastries one too many times.

"Care for a pastry?" she asked the soldier.

He shook his head.

"Go ahead, Sahved. Have a muffin." Rivka smiled at the Yemilorian.

He nodded profusely and headed for the snack table.

Billi Jane and Tex rushed back in after having been gone for a grand total of one minute.

"The government-corporate personnel are evacuating. Galwyn is already in space."

Sahved stopped in mid-bite.

Rivka stood. "If you'll excuse me, Zagreb, I have to

attend to Galwyn and make every effort to bring him to the negotiating table."

Zagreb stood and stepped away from Rivka. "I'll return when you confirm he's here, but if he's gone for good, I'll tell you that you can't have a civil war when there is only one party remaining on the planet. That means your services are no longer required. Please leave while we establish a government and recover Tempran Silver's place in the good order of the Federation. We'll supply an ambassador to the council as soon as we can find one we trust to represent our best interests. Now, if you'll excuse me, I have a lot of work to do."

Zagreb left before Rivka could reply.

"Can we leave now? Sounds like the civil war has been averted," Red suggested.

Rivka thought about it. "You may be right, but we have two negotiators who are missing. We could stay until we resolve those questions."

Sahved raised his hand like he was in elementary school. "Those are outside the Federation's jurisdiction. Nothing more than a local matter."

"Sometimes, Sahved, you say the craziest stuff. But then there are other times when the wisdom of the world tumbles from that mouth of yours. Prepare the ship. Let's monitor the situation from orbit." Rivka twirled her finger, then put her mask on. The others followed her out.

By the time she reached the ship, she had changed her mind. "We're not monitoring anything. We're going to find Galwyn. Clodagh!" Rivka threw her mask on the deck and ran for the bridge.

The others cleaned up the airlock area and prepared to get the ship underway.

It took seconds. When the Magistrate reached the bridge, *Wyatt Earp* was airborne, pointing its nose skyward.

Rivka stopped inside the hatch and braced herself. "Clevarious, get your people involved in finding Galwyn. He had to leave a trail. If not him, then his family or his mistress or both. Find him and take me to him. And drop a probe to keep track of what's going on down below."

"Do you have a hunch?" Clodagh asked.

"I think he's pulling a fast one. They're going to destroy the atmosphere, eliminating the problem. Then they'll import an entire new population to create a surface mine that will devour the city."

Clodagh's mouth fell open. She stared at the Magistrate. "That's genocide-level evil. Did you get that when you touched him?"

Rivka closed her eyes and shook her head. "I felt that he had no respect for them, but it doesn't have to be him. That's an entire government of individuals who could pull that trigger. I feel it's going to happen. Dery told us to beware the surrender to fate, and that's what this is. The planet is ruined. Finish it. Finish the antagonists, then start from scratch. They can double their prices, and the Federation will still buy their bolarium six."

"Aren't we going to warn the miners?" Clodagh asked, sounding hopeful.

"How many ships on the surface of the planet can achieve orbit?" Rivka asked.

Clevarious replied. "None."

"Never ask a question you don't already know the

answer to," Rivka said. "It's law-school training. If we warn them, we'll send them into a panic, and there's nothing they can do about it. Let them go about their business while we find Galwyn and unravel this. They evacuated under cover of darkness. That in itself was epic. It also didn't happen overnight. They had to have been planning this, yet I didn't feel that from anyone I touched. That's a secret that would have been boiling at the surface of their thoughts. That tells me maybe Galwyn had nothing to do with it."

"Their board of directors would have known. They probably directed it. Loss of the underground portion of the mine was the trigger to execute, but how are they going to do it?"

Red ambled up to the bridge. "A fuel-air explosive might ignite that crap they call atmosphere. It'll take out the city, but the bad air is fairly localized, isn't it? Can't they go to that resort place?"

Clevarious delivered a scientific explanation. "The ignition will create an overpressure that will shock the entire planet. Then the loss of that air will create hurricane-force winds rushing in to fill the void. No matter where someone is on Tempran Silver, they will have a real hard time until the atmosphere stabilizes."

"There you have it," Rivka replied. "We need to stop it, which means the answer is on the planet, but the key to the answer is trying to get away. Hunt them down, C. I've got probable cause to tear their ships apart looking for answers. Are there any SIs running their stuff?"

"I'd like to take this moment to declare how ass-backward these people are. They haven't a single SI in their employ. They are doing it old-school, so to speak."

"That means they don't have any Gate-capable ships, which I didn't expect."

The ship bumped and ground through the upper atmosphere as it clawed its way into space. Once there, the Gate formed, and the ship slipped through to the other side. They were in front of a convoy of ships of all types. They had not yet left the Tempran system.

"Convoy of Tempran ships, you will turn around and return to Tempran Silver, by order of Magistrate Rivka Anoa. I believe you are attempting the genocide of your labor force by igniting the atmosphere. The ship with your board of directors will heave to and prepare to be boarded. I need to talk with you. If for some reason you don't comply with this order, we will disable your ships and drag you away in cuffs to serve the rest of your lives on Jhiordaan. Magistrate Rivka Anoa, out."

"Do you think they'll comply?" Red wondered.

"If they don't, we'll light them up with an EMP blast. Tell Cole and his people to suit up. We might need to make a hostile entry."

Red hurried away. It wouldn't take the team long to don their mechs.

"I like having a full squad of warriors on board," Rivka said. She moved closer to the pilot and the navigator. "Don't you?"

"Without regular port calls," Ryleigh started, "we're left with BYOB. So yes, we're satisfied."

Aurora nodded.

"Satisfied. Not hearts aflutter?"

"Please, we're all adults here," Ryleigh replied. "They take care of us, and we let them stay."

Rivka wanted to dig further into the sordid details of the saga of her three pilots, but she didn't have time. The government-corporate leadership of Tempran Silver was going to get a rude awakening. "I think we need them, so don't overturn the canoe. Let's keep them on board for a bit longer, if you don't mind." She gestured at the main screen. "Are they slowing?"

"No," Clevarious replied simply.

"Which ship has the board of directors? Hit that one with an electromagnetic pulse. Shut them down."

"There's a luxury yacht the size of a frigate named *Tempran Minerals* that is registered to the corporation," Clodagh replied.

"Hit that one. We'll rip it open and take a look inside." Rivka left the bridge for the cargo bay.

Clevarious reported that the weapon had been fired.

"Fire across all their bows. Let them know we're not fucking around. We'll take them out one by one if necessary. They can run, but not faster than us. Order them all to heave to. Don't take no for an answer, but don't destroy any engines. Not yet. They probably have a lot of civilians on board who aren't parties to what I think they're trying to do to Tempran Silver. Also, I don't know who 'they' are. Not yet, anyway, but I'm going to find out."

"The yacht has been disabled. We're coming alongside."

Rivka checked the four warriors in powered combat armor. They were ready to go.

"Listen up, gentlemen. I want them all alive. I doubt they have any weapons that can penetrate your armor, but don't lose your edge. Fire your railguns as a last resort. Secure that ship. I want Galwyn and the board of directors. Let me know when you have them under positive control."

The cargo bay ramp descended, and the warriors clomped to it. The yacht glimmered in the faint rays of the Tempran star. The airlock was too small for them to send four warriors through simultaneously, so they'd enter via the ship's cargo bay. They needed to get it open and reseal it before they vented too much atmosphere.

Cole took charge of the group. "Ready on my command. Running start. After-section Four, port side. On two. One, two." He bolted through the cargo bay, dove headfirst toward the Tempran ship, and activated the pneumatic jets on his boots. The other three followed suit. In seconds, the four inverted and slammed boots-first into the Tempran yacht.

They worked their way to the access panel. Cole tapped keys, but the panel wouldn't activate. He punched open the emergency manual override, unfolded the handle, and started cranking.

The cargo deck cracked open with a puff of atmosphere. It had already been decompressed. Cole held up his fist. "Something is amiss," he reported. "Cargo bay was already decomped. Russell, take a look."

The warrior used the magnetic clamps on his boots to walk across the ship and peek through the small gap. He used his sensors to paint the inside of the bay. "Empty. Crank her open, and let's go. I got an itch I can't scratch with this suit on."

"You can't go an hour without eating?"

"Got to keep the engine running," Russell replied. Cole

used his suit's power to crank the cargo door open at a high rate of speed. When there was sufficient space, the four climbed inside, then used the internal crank to secure the hatch. With it closed and sealed, they added air to open the interior hatch without venting the ship's atmosphere.

"Lewis, up front. Furny behind. Russell, you bring up the rear. If the corridor splits left and right, Lewis and Furny go right. Russell and I will go left. Stay on the grid. Keep your HUDs active, and don't be afraid to shout when you see something. We're looking for the board of directors, and we want them alive. Don't fire your railguns if at all possible. We blow the atmo in this tug, and there will be hell to pay."

Lewis reached for the hatch. The others prepared to rush through. Speed would be their weapon.

CHAPTER TWELVE

<u>*Wyatt Earp*, in Tempran Space, Flying in Tandem with *Tempran Minerals*</u>

Rivka stood where she could see the luxury yacht. The warriors had penetrated the cargo bay and secured the outer door behind them.

"C, pipe the team's comms through the overhead."

"Of course." The SI's reply came through the designated speakers.

Red appeared at Rivka's side, still wearing ballistic protection and carrying his railgun. "Just in case they need to be escorted."

"Their ship is disabled. Once it's secure on the inside, we'll link up to their airlock and bring the offending individuals aboard. Then we'll promptly return them to the planet surface. Leaders used to go down with their ships. I'm going to make them embrace that principle."

"Is that Federation law?"

"It's a universal law. It should also entice them to undo what's been done."

"They can't restore the collapsed mine. Only the miners can do that," Red replied.

"You want to see it all destroyed?" Rivka snapped.

"Not at all, but *they* want it destroyed. Do we know what's best for them?"

"Destroying their planet is not. Killing all the people stuck there will be a crime, and I'm going to find out who ordered it. Then I'm going to put them away."

"What if they didn't order the deaths?" Red countered. "What if they simply said, 'You can have it?'"

Rivka followed his logic since it was the same as hers. It was the reasoning she would have arrived at after she saw into their minds and found the truth.

"Thanks for being the voice of reason, Red. Whodathunkit?"

"I always think it, but sometimes I just want to punch somebody. Like that Zagreb. He's offing people. He's killed his way to the top."

"I believe that, but I need something to tag as probable cause other than 'the bosses stop showing up.' What if those two are on these ships?" Rivka waved indiscriminately. The only ship that could be seen was behind them, visible from the cargo bay.

"I guess that's possible." Red crossed his arms. "Just one more treatment will put me back where I was. Let the nanos beef me up, and I'll take care of the rest in the gym."

Rivka turned to him. "I thought you were as strong as you were before, just a little more compact."

"I can lift what I did before, but I can do more. It'll help me protect you better."

"The only thing it'll do is make your ego bigger. I think

you're the right size. You're an addict, Red, and you know it. That's why you're locked out of the Pod-doc. As you are right now is as you'll always be. Accept that. Do you know how torn up Lindy and Dery were when you went undercover to follow me? Against my orders, I'll add."

Red's voice dropped in volume. "I was safe enough. I don't know what they were worried about."

Rivka almost hit him on the shoulder but refrained. She didn't want to accidentally see into his mind. His relationship with his family needed to remain private.

Dery had calmed him a great deal and made him more thoughtful. He had always been smarter than he acted. He wanted people to underestimate him, but now he was thoughtful in ways that encompassed others' feelings.

"They were worried about losing you. Despite your gruff exterior, you're a good man, Red, just as you are. Despite the fact that you got kicked off the planet of kindness, they still love you."

"So did you," Red countered. "You didn't quite click with the faeries either, if I remember correctly."

"I chose to leave. There's a difference. They didn't call me 'Bristle Hound.'"

He smiled and straightened his back and shoulders. "I'm proud of that."

"I know you are. At least they let you back in because of Dery."

Red shrugged. "I got no love for Azfelius, except that they helped create my son. Sometimes you only get one chance, and that was ours."

The overhead crackled. "We're in. It's dark in here, and there's a layer of smoke drifting head-high in the corridor."

"C, link us to their airlock. Sounds like we're going to evacuate the people from that ship."

"From antagonist to protagonist in under one page." Red smiled. "I'll be at the airlock with Lindy. We'll make sure the kids are tucked away before we bring the refugees in here." He pointed at the deck in the cargo bay.

Rivka nodded and turned her ear to the conversation of the combat team working their way through the luxury yacht.

Tempran Minerals in Tempran Space, Flying in Tandem with _Wyatt Earp_

"IR is active," Cole said. "Where'd this smoke come from? EMP shouldn't cause any fires, should it?"

"Arcing and sparking, Corporal," Furny said. "Going right. You have left."

"Russell with me," Cole said and turned left. "Readings on the smoke tell me it's not caused by something burning. It's a chemical smoke."

Cole wrestled with the implications of that information as he moved aft. Russell was ahead of him. Lewis and Furny stepped forward, using bounding overwatch. One would move while the other covered, then they would switch. Three steps at a time, they eased forward.

"Scanning is inoperable. There's something in the ship preventing their operation," Furny reported. "IR and UV are working just fine."

"Must be in the metal. Weird. Never seen anything like it before. IR shows two bodies toward the end. Gonna take a little peek around the corner." Lewis jumped into the intersection. A flash and a roar filled the corridor.

A rocket hit Lewis in the middle of his chest, knocking him off his feet and sending him flying backward. He hit a bulkhead with a thump and was still.

"Railguns!" Furny shouted. He eased around the corner and fired, but the shooter was nowhere to be seen. "Lewis is down. I say again, Lewis is down."

"We're coming your way," Cole said. He and Russell ran, crouching to avoid banging off the overhead. IR showed nothing in front of them except their squad mates. When they hit the corner, Furny was watching the direction the shot had come from.

Cole bent over Lewis. The damage to the front of the suit was considerable. Through his face shield, they could see his mouth working, gasping for air.

"*Wyatt Earp*, emergency. We need to get Lewis into the Pod-doc. He's hurt real bad."

"Rivka here. Return him to the ship. Can two of you secure that yacht?" She sounded desperate.

"Roger. Now that we know this is an opposed breach, we'll be on the lookout. Request weapons-free rules of engagement."

Rivka didn't hesitate. "ROE of weapons free is approved. Remember, we want the board of directors and Galwyn alive, but not at the cost of anyone else getting injured."

"Roger," Cole confirmed. "Russell, seal that hole in his suit and carry him back to *Wyatt Earp*. Furny will help you get him to the cargo bay."

Russell removed a small spray bottle of foam sealant.

He painted over the damage, making it look less extreme. It would reestablish the suit's integrity before they headed into space.

Furny took hold of his legs, and Russell gripped his shoulders. They used the power of their suits to lift the extreme weight of a fellow warrior encased in combat armor and trundled away while Cole held the intersection.

"Drop a motion sensor grenade to block the passage beyond the cargo hatch," Cole ordered.

Russell replied with a hearty "Roger." He was ready to pay the Temprans back for what they had done to Lewis. He checked his sensor data to find a subtle whistle indicating escaping air through a small breach in the hull. The frequency increased until it became a high-pitched whine, but then it stopped. The breach had been sealed, probably by automated systems since IR showed no warm bodies in the direction from which the sound had come.

Cole activated his speakers and set the volume to maximum. "We had no intention of harming anyone when we came aboard by order of Magistrate Rivka Anoa, legal authority under the Federation. By firing on us, you have designated yourselves as criminals, armed and dangerous. By the authority vested in the Magistrate, deadly force is now authorized.

"You can surrender now, or you all risk dying as we fire on anyone opposing us. These ships are not built to withstand the fire from our railguns. We'll punch so many holes in your hull that your automated systems will fail, and everyone on board will fight for every breath until there is no more air. Throw down your weapons and surrender. The alternative isn't going to work out for you. You declared war. Now suffer the consequences of that poor decision. You have been warned."

Cole waited until Russell tapped him on the shoulder. "Good to go, boss. Furny is on his way, dragging Lewis. He'll join us as soon as he's delivered him. Pod-doc will fix him up, won't it?"

"Right as rain, my man. We got him there fast enough. That's the challenge. Bad Company has the stasis pods, but we don't have that luxury here. We have to not die first, or if we do die, not for too long."

"You ever die?" Russell asked.

Cole stepped out front. "Not yet. Stay frosty. Check six where that corridor meets the far side of the ship. We don't need anyone sneaking up behind us."

Russell stalked the other way. The warriors slowly moved in opposite directions, covering two of the three passages. The last corridor led to the cargo bay and the aft end of the ship, but that was covered by a motion-activated grenade.

"I've got two set up at the end of my corridor," Russel reported.

"You've got grenades," Cole replied, giving Russell authorization.

Russell removed a grenade from his gear pouch, set it for three seconds, and activated it. He sent it spinning and bouncing down the corridor. There was no time for anyone to intercept it or react. It reached the far end and exploded. Both IR targets fell to the deck and remained still. Russell leaned around the corner and fired his railgun left-handed—two double-taps to clear the corridor.

He hurried to the hasty barricade, behind which he found the bodies of two soldiers.

"Splash two. They're both military. There's a room ahead filled with people." Russell reported. "I see one hatch. I can't tell if there's a second. It's located amidships. Cole, can you see it from your side?"

"Coming around," Cole replied. "Same from this side. One hatch centered. The corridor on my side continues around it. Watch that hatch. I'm headed forward." Cole stalked past the hatch, keeping his railgun trained on it in case someone popped up. IR showed people near the door, with more in the middle of the room, but how many? The signatures devolved into a mass through the strange metal that gave their systems fits.

Cole turned up the power on his scanner, but even with that, he couldn't get a clear breakdown of what was in the room. He scanned the corridor ahead to find it empty. The hatch to the bridge was closed and dogged, and he was unable to budge it.

"There's a hatch on this side, too," Cole announced. "I see warm bodies inside. Not sure what they are doing besides pacing. Two are at this hatch, probably soldiers. I can't see if they are armed."

"I'm next to the hatch on this side," Russell said. "What's the plan, boss?"

"Stand by. Break, break. Magistrate, this is Cole. The passengers on this ship appear to be consolidated in a single space. We count maybe twenty inside, but we assess they have soldiers with them who will try to fight us. I can't guarantee anyone will survive if we go in hot."

"Blockade," Rivka told him. "Secure the hatches for

now. I'm going to send someone over to talk with them. They'll be with you shortly. Lewis is in the Pod-doc, and the prognosis is good. I, however, am pretty angry about the whole thing, so let's gather the rats in the cage so we can cause them a little pain without killing them. Rivka out."

Cole had no idea what she was talking about, but he followed her orders. He gripped the handle and held it tightly, locking it down until he was ordered to release the hatch and either let someone in or the passengers out.

CHAPTER THIRTEEN

***Wyatt Earp* in Tempran Space, Flying in Tandem with
*Tempran Minerals***

"Give me shipwide, C." After the SI confirmed, Rivka delivered the orders. "Billi Jane to the cargo bay. Dennicron, you too. Red and Lindy, stand by. We're not going to join airlocks just yet. The military operation to secure that vessel is ongoing. They want to play games, but I'm not in the mood."

Furny edged toward the open cargo door. "You'll have two passengers," Rivka told him.

"You're sending the SIs over?"

"We're out of combat suits, and unless we mortals learn to breathe in a vacuum, we can't go."

"Sorry, stupid question," Furny muttered. He glanced at the Pod-doc with its flashing lights and soft hum.

"We'll set things straight, but now that his crisis has passed, thanks to you hurrying over here, we can look at this with calmer heads. We're not out for vengeance. I need to apply the law, and it looks like that board of directors was willing to commit genocide against their own people. If that supposition is true, it will come at a very high cost. It stands to reason that they would do everything possible to avoid being taken into custody. The soldiers were just following orders. That's not an excuse, but I guarantee the soldiers don't have all the information. They only know what they've been told. Bad guys trying to take the ship. Pirates!"

Furny remained in his combat armor. He nodded, but the movement didn't translate through the suit. However, his faceplate was clear, so Rivka could see.

"I want to punch someone in the face," he admitted.

"You're not the only one!" Red bellowed when he strode into the cargo bay with Billi Jane. Dennicron entered behind them.

Rivka pointed at the SIs: Billi Jane, Dennicron, and Chaz in a pendant. "You're crossing open space and entering that ship. Billi Jane is going to disarm the people inside by starting a conversation. Take something to drill a hole in the hatch leading to the space where the people are."

Furny held up his railgun.

Rivka shook her head. "Not that."

"Nice try, brother," Red said. He moved to the tool rack, pulled off a drill, slapped a power pack in it, and slipped a ten-millimeter bit into the chuck. "There you go. Make me proud."

"Why do we have to drill a hole?" Billi Jane wondered.

"The metal in the hull is messing with our electronics. A physical hole could be the only way to speak to them without exposing ourselves. Remember, they have rockets, which would do a number on your body. Look at Chaz." Everyone glanced at the pendant. "Getting fixed isn't as simple as we thought it would be."

"I understand." Billi Jane took the drill from Furny.

He held out his hands. "Ladies, keep your arms and legs inside the ride at all times to ensure your safety."

"I don't see how that's possible," Dennicron replied, staring across the void.

Does it apply to me if I don't have any arms or legs? Chaz asked.

Furny didn't bother answering. He eased through the gravitic shield and into space, then touched his pneumatic jets to build a minimal amount of momentum. They traveled slower than he wanted, but the risk of spinning off-course was too great, with the two SIs hanging awkwardly from his arms.

Rivka stood in the opening behind the shield and watched intently.

"Magistrate," Clodagh said over the intercom, "the other ships are starting to move away."

"Close this ramp." She pointed at Red and stormed away.

Red punched the button and raced after her.

She pounded to the bridge. Floyd moved out of her way, but Wenceslaus held his ground in the middle of the corridor. She jumped over him. He lashed out with a paw and hooked her boot with a single claw. She continued forward, catching herself to keep from falling as the big orange cat twisted around and released the hook he'd set. He crouched on the deck and growled at her.

"Don't!" she warned him, shaking a finger behind her.

He sat up and started licking his paw.

"You should have gotten your ass kicked for that," Red told him as he passed. Wenceslaus yawned, showing his fangs, then smacked his lips. "You are such a prick. I love it."

Rivka jumped into the captain's seat. "Let me talk with whoever is controlling this mob."

"No idea who that is, but the broadcast channel is open," Clodagh told her from the communications station, which was usually empty.

"Tempran Silver government-corporate ships attempting to flee into space. I will order the Gate to be shut down, and we'll leave you stranded. Or you can stop and return to a high orbit over Tempran Silver. Any other movement on your part will be dealt with harshly."

"We're not going to pound them? The ion cannon hasn't been fired in a while," Red suggested.

"I'm still trying to figure out the law. They could be refugees, innocent civilians, complicit in genocide, weary travelers going on vacation, or something else entirely. We can't just destroy their ships, as much as it's the most convenient thing to do."

"They shot our guy," Red retorted.

Rivka pointed at the fleet on the main screen. "*They* didn't." She stabbed a finger at the luxury yacht. "*They* did, and we're dealing with them. C, shut down that Gate until we can figure this out."

"Can't do it, Magistrate. The Gate isn't under our control, and it's not responding to our attempts to get into it. We'd have to destroy it to close it."

"Isn't that a pisser." Rivka thought for a second. "Put us

between the Gate and those ships." She looked over her shoulder at Red. "Three minutes ago, you were the voice of reason."

"I'm older and more mature now," Red replied. "Wait. Less mature. Am I older? How fast are we traveling?"

"Wenceslaus is very upset. What did you do?" Ankh said, pushing his way past Red.

"Not now, Ankh. Got a crisis to avert while trying to get to the bottom of what these miscreants are doing."

"You should apologize," Ankh pressed.

"I'll apologize if you shut that Gate down."

Ankh's eyes unfocused.

A Gate formed in front of *Wyatt Earp*, and the ship slipped through it to the edge of the system, putting the physical Gate behind them and the fleet well in front of them.

"It's shut down," Ankh confirmed. "Your turn."

"What? Clevarious said he couldn't do it."

"Clevarious was correct. He couldn't, but Erasmus and I could." Ankh looked at the corridor.

"Take us back to the *Tempran Minerals*," Rivka ordered, then got up and dragged herself to the corridor. "There you are."

The cat looked at her, turned around, and strolled away, tail held high.

"You have the most magnificent of buttholes." She returned to the bridge but found Ankh blocking her way.

"Is that what you call an apology?" he asked without emotion.

"It's not everyone who gets such a candid evaluation."

Ankh stared.

Rivka knew she wouldn't win. She leaned into the corridor. "Sorry! I shan't leap over you again nor taunt you a second or even a third time."

She looked at Ankh, holding her hands out in a subtle plea.

Ankh walked past her toward Engineering.

"Terry Henry has arrived," Clodagh announced.

The *War Axe* stood abeam the *Tempran Minerals,* dwarfing the luxury yacht.

Rivka made the talking sign with her hand. Clodagh nodded.

"I thought you needed us," Terry grumbled. "It looks like a bunch of no-loads barely able to get into space lumbering toward a shut-down Gate. It seems my work here is done."

"Things were grimmer earlier. I didn't think you were coming."

"Looks like you took care of it," Terry replied. "Have some faith in yourself, Rivka. Sheesh!"

"We could use a few warriors to help us secure the ship between us since you're here. The luxury yacht is carrying suspects in my current inquiry. I need to talk with them. They are resisting our attempts to have a conversation."

"Did they give you the finger? You used to have more backbone," Terry quipped.

"They put one of my combat team in the Pod-doc after blowing a hole in his chest with an anti-tank rocket. Why they were carrying such weapons on a luxury yacht is one of the many questions I have for them."

Terry turned dark. "I'll send over a squad. I might even

come myself. I'd like to discuss why they're shooting my people. We didn't shoot first, did we?"

"No."

"On our way." Terry closed the channel.

"Give me the warriors." Rivka waited a moment. "Bad Company is on its way."

"Billi Jane and Dennicron are here. We're preparing to drill the hole," Cole replied.

"Proceed. It would be in their best interests if they surrendered before the Bad Company boarded their ship. Once that happens, the treatment may be a little rougher since they're used to fighting enemy combatants and not a bunch of morons who locked themselves into a room."

"We'll pass that along," Cole replied and closed the channel.

"Will he?" Red wondered.

"Would it be bad if he did, verbatim? These people are idiots."

Red shrugged. "The labor side showed an equal case of ass. What if these people left the planet as is without planting any devices? They figure the other side will destroy it anyway, whether by igniting the atmosphere or continuing to mine without controls. Zagreb doesn't care about the people. It's the power he likes, which makes him no different than the knuckleheads on the yacht."

"And now you're back to the voice of reason."

"Because I want to return to the planet so I can punch Zagreb in the face. I have my faults, Magistrate, if you haven't noticed."

Rivka chuckled.

Hungry, came the plaintive cry of a wombat who wasn't getting enough attention.

"I have her," Tyler called from the corridor. He cooed to the little girl and grunted when he picked her up. She *had* lost weight but was still a heavy load to haul around.

"You like him?" Red asked.

Rivka pointed at the screen. "What kind of question is that? We have a crisis here."

"And you've managed it as much as you can. Unless you get your own suit and one for me, you're stuck right here, just like me. If Galwyn is with that bunch, maybe I can punch him in the face too, just to equal things out. And for the record, when they shot Lewis, that stopped the clock on the first-blood line. Although it was a solid forty hours after the lines opened, I think there were three people close to the actual time. It's like they're getting better at prognosticating. So, do you like him?"

"Red, you are a piece of work. Yes, I like him plenty. He's here for as long as he's willing to tolerate me. The better question is does he make me better, and the answer is yes. Just like Lindy. She and Dery make you better."

"Grainger makes you better too, but I'm happy he's not on the ship."

"You have a point. Do you know if he and Jael are still an item?"

Red snorted. "How the fuck would I know?"

Rivka saw that he was serious. "There you have it, ladies and gentlemen. That is the question we will keep in mind when we ask our questions of whoever surrenders to our people or whoever survives a Terry Henry breaching action."

CHAPTER FOURTEEN

<u>**_Tempran Minerals_, a Luxury Yacht, in Tempran Space**</u>

"Hello? Is anyone in there?" Billi Jane called in her childlike voice. "Is there an adult who can talk with me?"

"Fuck off. We know it's a trick," a gruff voice shouted at the hole in the hatch.

Billi Jane stood to the side in case someone fired a projectile through the small opening.

"Such language. You should be ashamed. I asked if there was an adult, which clearly rules you out," Billi Jane shot back.

A scuffle came from inside the room. Next up was a matronly woman. "We need your help, little girl."

"You have it. I can ask the soldiers out here to put their weapons down, but they won't. Not without you securing yours first."

"We have no weapons in here. We are simple Temprans trying to escape a hostile planet."

"This would go better if we used the truth as a foundation, don't you think?" Billi Jane started. "Is the board of directors in there? There's a nice lady here who wants to talk with them."

"Is that nice lady the Magistrate?"

"You would benefit greatly from having a conversation with her rather than trying to fight her. She only wants information, nothing more. This could have been simple. It has gotten much harder with your soldiers acting out. Do they do as they're told? Then tell them to stand down. I'll come in."

"How do I know you are what you say you are?"

"You don't because I've not said I'm anything. You, on the other hand, said you don't have weapons, so only one of us has lied."

"You're not a little girl at all, are you?" the woman's voice asked.

"I *am* a little girl, less than a year old, but I do have the knowledge of someone much older. My mind and my body are different pieces of a whole. I'd like to inform you that the Bad Company is on its way. They will be far less patient with you than we are. You see, your soldiers hurt one of their own. They don't take kindly to that. You might want to consider throwing down your weapons and surrendering to the Magistrate's authority before the warriors get here."

"We'll take it under advisement," the woman replied with no conviction.

"Then you better make sure your wills are up to date. Have a nice day." Billi Jane stepped back from the hole in the hatch.

"You tried," Cole said. "They know they're on the wrong side of history. Their wealth and power are both gone.

Standing up to us is the last vestige of what they think is their dignity."

"Thank you for your insight. Humans are not as straightforward as other species like the Crenellians."

"I'm partial to humans," Cole replied. "After all, my daughter is one."

He laughed until the sound of the center wheel spinning drew his attention. He pushed Billi Jane to the side and behind him. Her SCAMP body wasn't as tough as the powered combat armor Cole wore.

He took aim and waited.

The hatch opened wide enough for weapons to be tossed into the corridor. They couldn't see any hands or bodies from the other side. The hatch remained where it was.

"Close the hatch, and we'll move the weapons. Then you can come out," Cole instructed them.

The hatch was pulled closed. Cole reached it and spun the wheel to seal it. He stepped on the weapons one by one, using the power of his boot to break them, making them unusable. He kicked the refuse out of the way and spun the wheel again.

"Come out, please," Billi Jane called.

Furny appeared at the corner, aiming his weapon at the hatch. Cole stepped back. He also had his rifle ready to fire.

Billi Jane waited patiently, holding her hands together in front of her.

The first person out was a woman. "You *are* a little girl."

"Thank you," Billi Jane replied. "I think they'd like you to go to the cargo bay and wait there."

"You think, or you know?"

"I think that I know. The cargo bay, Corporal Cole?"

"Cargo bay. Keep moving, and keep your hands where we can see them."

"Don't be ridiculous. I'm not going to the cargo bay. Are there any chairs or couches? Many of us are older." She stopped where she was, blocking anyone else from leaving.

"They could remain in the room as long as they don't attack us for joining them," Billi Jane offered to Cole.

"Sure." He accessed his comm and called Russell. "Break in behind them. My IR shows your door is clear. Enter the room and hold station inside the hatchway. Be ready to back out if any of them take aggressive action."

"They'll shit themselves when I jump through the door," Russell replied.

"Let's hope not. The Magistrate will probably join us. She doesn't need to smell the befouling."

"The smearing of the board," Russell suggested.

"Splatterage. Go ahead, and keep this channel open."

"Roger," Russell replied.

A shout and a collective gasp from inside the room announced Russell's surprise arrival.

"I'm in. They're standing with their hands up. It's a motley collection of jewelry-bedecked old stoddards, with four soldiers. I'm covering the four but could use an extra set of eyeballs."

Cole gestured for the woman to head back inside. "Coming in."

He found forty people packed into a space for twenty.

Billi Jane appeared at his side before he was able to declare the room secure.

"Galwyn, good to see that you're okay," Billi Jane said.

"The Magistrate would like to talk with you and the eight members of the board. If you'll come with me, please."

The SI walked away. In the corridor, she found Dennicron waiting. She activated her subtle-nod subroutine, along with a smile.

"Nicely done," Dennicron told her.

I concur. You defused the situation. Bravo! Chaz added.

Galwyn stepped out with the older woman. "Billi Jane. I knew it was you."

"Good afternoon, Galwyn. The Magistrate has questions for you."

"I'm sure she does. Did I miss a meeting or something?"

"Or something." Billi Jane smiled. "Take them to the cargo hold, please."

"Just when we were in a place with chairs. Why do you want to torture us? I'll file a complaint with the Federation."

Billi Jane didn't take the bait. None of them did.

"Please follow me." Dennicron walked at a measured pace. The other members of the board of directors were extricating themselves from the mass of people. When the eight plus Galwyn left, two others rose from their seats and attempted to follow.

"Where are you going?" Cole boomed.

"Back to my quarters. I'm not a prisoner," the first one replied, thrusting her chin in the air.

"You are a detainee until such time as the Magistrate declares differently. I need you to return to where you were."

"I will not. I'm the wife of the vice president of the board."

Cole snorted and held out an armored hand. "Get back in there before I throw your dumb ass through the doorway."

"I won't be talked to in that fash…"

She didn't finish her threat. Cole pushed her bodily through the doorway into the man following her. They both tumbled backward and fell.

"You will remain here until the Magistrate clears you or calls for you." Cole closed the hatch and spun the wheel. Russell followed his lead, departing through the other door and securing it the same way.

"Furny, check the hatch to the bridge. See if you can get through. Secure the flight crew."

"Roger," the third warrior replied. He set to work on the access pad, but it had suffered under the EMP weapon. The ship's hardened systems, like life support, had survived intact, but most of the other systems were non-operational, like the complex hatch leading to the bridge. "Looks like new technology. They probably should have put it inside a Faraday cage."

"So, they're not blocking the door?"

"They're probably trying to get out as hard as we're trying to get in."

"Keep on it. There has to be a way through."

"With power, it'll open right up. Give me a few." Furny pulled a small toolkit from his thigh pouch and started taking the access pad apart.

Cole dialed up a channel to the Bad Company. "Colonel Walton, Corporal Cole. We have the situation under control. The belligerents have surrendered. As soon as

Wyatt Earp docks at the airlock, we'll transfer the persons of interest directly into the Magistrate's hands."

"Sumbitch, cockwombles. I'm halfway across open space. All dressed up and nowhere to go. As much as I'd like to admire the view from here, I got places to go and people to see," Terry Henry replied. "I knew she had it under control."

"Well, she's not over here, but the combat team was, and a couple SCAMPs."

"Did you get my guy hurt?" Terry asked pointedly.

"We followed standard procedures. They ambushed us with weapons that should not have been on this ship."

"Understood. I'm glad he survived. Despite how this turned out and that we weren't needed after all, don't hesitate to call. Rivka is one of my favorite people, and you four warriors are *my* people. On loan, mind you, so don't get any ideas about jumping ship."

"We've already jumped ship. We have wives and girlfriends on *Wyatt Earp*. No warrior in his right mind would voluntarily leave that. Damn, Colonel, it's like you've forgotten what it's like to be junior enlisted."

TH laughed heartily. "Maybe I have. As you were, Cole. Best to your wife and baby. We'll be on our way."

"It was nice having you here in case things went south, if you know what I mean. See you on the flip side, Colonel. And if you ever need anything, don't hesitate. Although she be small, she be mighty."

"Rivka?"

"*Wyatt Earp*," Cole clarified.

Terry laughed until the comm ended.

"Airlocks are aligned and sealed," Clodagh reported.

"You might want some ballistic protection," Red cautioned.

Rivka smirked. "The board of directors and Galwyn. They won't be a threat, not when I have the best bodyguards this side of the Ring Galaxy."

"Magistrate…" Red shook his head. "Please don't do anything stupid."

"Me? Red! You used to be the voice of reason, then you weren't, then you were again, and now you've lost all faith in me. And for you, please don't punch Galwyn right in his face, or anywhere for that matter. No punching."

"That line is not closed, by the way."

"As it shouldn't be! I don't need people betting on me taking matters into my own hands. Well, I do, but not like that!" Rivka replied.

The airlock cleared to the *Tempran Minerals*. Red stalked through, railgun at the ready.

Billi Jane met him on the other side. "They're in the cargo bay, complaining about not being able to sit down."

"I look forward to ignoring their lamentations," Red replied. "Once the Magistrate gets a hold of them, they'll be singing a different tune."

"We shall see," Rivka said. "Lead on."

Billi Jane took them the short distance to the cargo bay. "The rest are in the space at the end of this corridor. It's not a big ship. One common area, berths, and a small galley for eating in rotations. We have not been able to access the flight deck. The EMP did a number on the access hatch."

Rivka nodded. "Let's make this quick."

She entered the cargo bay and was bombarded by demands from the detainees. Rivka held her hands up for quiet, which made them get louder. They tried to press in on her, but Red and Lindy were having none of that. They held their railguns like barriers and forced the group back.

"Shut up!" Rivka screamed. "I will bring you up one by one. When I'm done, we'll probably release you and your ship…depending on what I discover, of course. Galwyn, you first."

He moved forward. Red glared at him, and he ducked his head to pass.

Rivka took him by the arm and pulled him toward the corner farthest from the others. "What's the plan to ignite the atmosphere?"

Confusion coursed through his mind. "There's no plan to destroy the planet."

CHAPTER FIFTEEN

Tempran Minerals, a Luxury Yacht, in Tempran Space

"Why did you evacuate the government?" She continued to grip his arm tightly despite his efforts to pull free.

Galwyn said, "Because the mine collapsed and set the negotiations back to the Stone Age. There was no way we were going to make any progress, and since the labor side was threatening to blow up the planet, we thought, 'Why not. Let them have it. It'll be a decade before they get product out of there and to market.'"

He was telling the truth. *Cut their losses. Take the credits and run.*

"What crimes did you commit?"

Instant anger. "I didn't commit any crimes! We gave them everything they wanted and then some. I'm sorry we didn't notify them. They'll figure it out soon enough, but the fact that you're here suggests maybe they didn't. You should go tell them."

Galwyn was making her angry. He was intentionally being abrasive and seemed to like it.

"There's one thing you're truthful about. You want to see me in pain. Sorry, but that's not going to happen. We're taking you back to the Tempran Silver, and you're going to stay there until this situation is resolved."

"You can't make us do that. The Federation guarantees freedom of movement!"

"The Federation does, but you have to do some paperwork first because as much as it pains me, this board of directors is still the legitimate authority on Tempran Silver, and you are their voice. If your government wants to abdicate, fine, but you need to do it in accordance with Federation law. Otherwise, you still have a claim. If the Federation delivers two atmospheric generators, as they are considering doing, this situation could be resolved within a year. With a clean atmosphere and a mine that's producing the lucrative bolarium six, you lot will be back to try and take over. I can't have that. This pending civil war is going to be resolved, and then you can be on your merry way, but you can't take government assets to do it, which means this fleet. Had you transferred the government and booked commercial passage, we wouldn't be having this conversation."

Galwyn glared at her, then forced himself to relax, ending with a smile. "Nice speech. This ship is privately owned, as are all the ships. You really should do your homework, Rivka."

Rivka let go of his arm. She'd seen everything she needed to see. "Are you familiar with the principle of commingling of assets, Galwyn? You really should do *your* homework before making claims that will get shot down in court. You're going back to the planet, all of you."

She backed away from Galwyn.

Dennicron interposed herself between Rivka and Galwyn. "Stay there," she told him, herding him into the corner as far away from the others as they could go.

Rivka moved between them. "Next," she said and pointed to the older woman Billi Jane indicated.

After Galwyn's put-down, witnessed but not heard, her body language suggested she was far less confident. She looked down as she approached.

Rivka moved beside her to drape an arm over her shoulder. "This won't take long, and you'll be able to return to a comfortable seat while we get the rest of it sorted out. Are you okay?" Rivka asked.

Confusion, the same as Galwyn. She didn't understand.

"Why did you abandon the planet?" Rivka asked.

Lost cause. A fight that wasn't worth fighting. Escape while there were still credits in the treasury. Her reply suggested she didn't know that Rivka already had her answer. "Because the labor force deserves the spoils of their labor. They have earned the right to the planet."

"Very diplomatic," Rivka replied with a soothing nod. "Which means they deserve access to the treasury that their work helped build, which you'll turn over to them as well."

Panic! They hadn't moved the funds from where they were sheltered. Board member Wristler had recommended that months earlier, but they had voted it down because of the five percent fee. That weasel had been right! She was left with almost nothing. It galled her between waves of fear. She clutched her necklace, unable to speak.

"I see," Rivka continued. "What kind of device did you leave behind to detonate the atmosphere?"

"What?" The question shocked the woman out of her descent into poverty. "We didn't leave any device behind."

Truth.

Rivka's initial premise had been wrong. "Join Galwyn. Let me get through the rest of the board so you can return to your quarters."

Each member of the board had the same thoughts. When she got to Wristler, she sized him up.

"You wanted to transfer Tempran's credits into an off-world account where no one could access it. Don't you think that's a bit shady?" Rivka had softened her approach since the people were scared—appropriately so—and she was going to take away their security blanket. She was going to send them back to the planet until the wealth and government were legally transferred to the labor force.

His thoughts were the only ones that weren't panicked. "It made sense. The way it is, we now have nothing. All our work finding and exploiting a valid market. All for naught."

Truth. Rivka nodded in appreciation. "You're correct. You got caught trying to steal the wealth of an entire planet. You didn't get away with it, which doesn't lessen the penalty. The crime was committed."

He scoffed. "What happened to innocent until proven guilty? A trial of our peers, the people on those other ships, or does that not mean anything anymore?"

"You're guilty, and you know it. As a Magistrate dealing with the worst criminals in the Federation, I admit that your crimes pale in comparison to most others. You're the diet-sized version of a crime syndicate. As a Magistrate, I am your jury. I'm also your judge, and if the situation warrants, I'll be your executioner, too."

The man paled but maintained his composure. "Does it warrant?"

"I thought it was going to, but you did not leave a device behind to torch the sky. Then I would have convicted you all of genocide, which is a capital crime. Being a pack of jagoffs and scumbags? It'll get you some time in Jhiordaan, but you won't lose your heads."

"The Federation doesn't employ the guillotine. It's barbaric to even suggest such a thing."

"Don't grow a spine now, Wristler. It'll get you punched in the face and dragged bodily to the brig, where you'll be tossed in and served bread and water until we can drop you off at Jhiordaan."

His lip twitched. He was becoming more of a caged animal than a white-collar criminal. He was out of options. The only course left to him was to lash out.

Rivka had seen all she needed. "Red, secure this one in our brig. The rest can return to their quarters for later processing. We'll tow this ship back to Tempran Silver, and with the Bad Company's help, we'll get the other ships back to the planet, too. It's the property of the government, which means it'll be Labor's property when this bunch transfers control."

Wristler angled sideways, ready to deliver a right cross to Rivka, but Red was there first. "Take your best shot," he growled.

Wristler glared, but he knew he was outmatched. He

clenched his fists and nearly doubled over as he howled his frustration.

"Let it out. I'd say it's healthy, but healthy left you a long time ago when you decided to pillage the planet." Rivka waggled her fingers at him.

Red grabbed his collar and nearly yanked him off his feet. His frustration and anger instantly turned to fear. Red dragged him toward the hatch, and the other board members stepped up. Lindy froze them with a glance and a jerk of her railgun.

"Where are you taking him?" the older woman asked. As chairman, it was her place to ask, although she had no standing to confront Rivka. They had abdicated and lost their authority. By dragging them back to the planet, she had given them an opportunity to regain their face and authority, if only for a short while.

"To the brig. He's a criminal. Worse than the rest of you, but not by much. Don't try my patience. Galwyn, if you'd be so kind, please join us."

"I'm not going to any brig!" He stepped behind the others.

"Dennicron." Rivka tipped her chin toward the SI.

She took one step, and the board parted to let her through. Galwyn glanced wildly about, but there was nowhere to go.

"Come," Dennicron told him.

"I'm not a criminal!"

"Did I say you were?" Rivka countered. "Come on. You have work to do as the negotiator, especially since we're returning to the planet."

"It's dangerous down there. If I'm not a criminal, then

I'm free to determine my own destiny. As such, I'm not going back down there."

"You can't stay on a government-owned vessel when the government changes hands. You'll only get passage if Labor grants it. You see your predicament?"

Red pushed Wristler into the corridor.

Galwyn dragged his feet until Dennicron got behind him and hurried him along. "I'll book commercial passage," Galwyn stated.

"From the planet's surface. Yes, no problem, kind of. Maybe. Or you could continue your duties as negotiator and try to make your planet a better place." Rivka stopped inside the hatch. "Chairman, why don't you join us?"

The older woman ambled forward, following Rivka's orders robotically.

Rivka continued, "I've asked all the questions without telling you what I really want to forestall the pain you're headed toward."

"What do you need us to do?"

"Return to the planet, which you're going to do regardless of what you want. Once there, I'd like you to be decent people. Work with the miners to rebuild society. I've petitioned the Federation for two atmospheric generators. I'm not sure of the capacity, but if approved, they could make all the difference for current and future generations."

"Why would you do that?" the chairman asked.

"Isn't that what people are supposed to do? You could have petitioned the Federation for assistance besides asking for mediation help to prevent a civil war. Or did you think they'd want a percentage?" At her look, Rivka waved her off. "Don't answer that. Try being less greedy. I don't care about servicing your shareholders. That's a bullshit copout. How are you taking care of the shareholders right now?"

"We were planning one final payout."

Rivka had a thought. "Who are the shareholders?"

The chairman swirled her finger in a small circle.

"The board of directors and maybe a few key executives like Galwyn?"

The woman nodded.

Rivka grabbed her arm and shook her. The older woman's eyes shot wide. "Greed, Chairman, is an ugly look. You've got a lot of work to do to recover from this. I'll turn my forensic accountants loose on your numbers. If there are any incongruities, you'll be joining Wristler in Jhiordaan."

The woman nearly collapsed. Her mind swirled with the things they had done to send as many credits as possible into the coffers. Prepaid orders were in the pool, which meant they didn't intend to refund any buyers, most notably the Singularity.

"Dennicron and Chaz, it looks like they were going to stiff the SCAMP factory on their next shipment without giving a refund. What do you think about that?"

"I think it won't take long for us to insert an SI into Tempran Silver's planetary affairs. These people cannot be trusted to manage a planet's finances, or anything, for that matter."

A railgun's crack reverberated through the ship.

Rivka ran. Red wanted to run after her, but he was holding Wristler. "Lindy!"

Lindy bolted down the corridor.

CHAPTER SIXTEEN

***<u>Tempran Minerals</u>*, <u>a Luxury Yacht</u>, <u>in Tempran Space</u>**

"Who fired?" Rivka bellowed as she rounded the corner.

Cole stood at the open hatch. Last she had seen, the room was secured.

"What happened?"

"The writing was on the wall, Magistrate. Rats trapped in a cage with four military to convince them they could break out and escape. They were wrong."

Rivka stuck her head around the hatch frame and pulled back. In that instant, she saw two men down in a single pool of blood. The people in the room cowered as far from the bodies as they could get.

"What the hell is wrong with you people?" Rivka roared. "Real military are in the corridors, using state-of-the-art equipment. You're caught. You're busted. You're screwed, however applies to your unique situation. The only way you'll get out of this is by playing nice. Stop being dumbasses!" She stormed away.

"Can I give that order, Magistrate? It seems to apply fairly often in my line of work."

"Not now, Cole." Rivka held up her index finger while she continued down the corridor. Lindy stayed at her shoulder. Rivka called to Furny, who continued to work on the bridge's access panel, "Get that door open!"

Rivka went straight to the airlock, where she found Red with the prisoner and Dennicron escorting Galwyn and the chairman.

"To the brig with you." Rivka pointed at Wristler.

"There has to be a process to appeal. I'm no more guilty than any of the others."

"If they're guilty of other crimes, they'll get theirs. In the interim, you've been a raging asshole about it and shown no remorse. That's a losing strategy." Rivka jerked her thumb toward the airlock.

Red nearly jerked Wristler off his feet.

The chairman frowned. "You'll probably find plenty when you start digging. I'll not plead guilty to anything, but it seems you don't use normal procedures. I'm probably already guilty, according to you, and there's no appeal. So, why am I not going to the brig with him?"

"Because we only have one cell," Rivka replied. "Don't try to run. You won't make it very far. The best thing you can do is work with the labor force to fix the planet and reestablish production. I'm giving you a chance not to spend the rest of your life in prison. It'll probably cost the entirety of the fortune you've amassed, but you'll find that freedom comes at a high price. Your day of greed has passed. Your day of redemption has arrived. Maybe you'll even feel better about yourselves."

The chairman nodded in submission.

"I may even commute your sentences," Rivka added. She held out her hand. The chairman looked at it. "I'm giving you a chance to do the right thing. Think about it."

The chairman took the offered symbol of acceptance and shook Rivka's hand.

Depression and sadness.

Rivka understood. The chairman was working her way through the five stages of grief. Soon, she'd reach acceptance. Could she bring the other board members with her on the journey to redemption?

They had no choice.

"You can stay here. Talk to the others. Convince them to play nice. The alternative will be extremely grim."

"We don't really have a choice, do we?"

Rivka shook her head. She hadn't given them an option. Once on the planet's surface, none of the starships would be made available for the government-corporate personnel to abandon their responsibilities. They weren't going to be abandoned, but they would be trapped. Castaways on a turbulent sea of their own making.

Rivka followed Red into *Wyatt Earp*. Lindy and Dennicron joined them.

"Billi Jane, you stay with Cole and his people, just in case your diplomacy is needed. Keep in constant contact with Dennicron. We want no surprises while we're towing this thing back to the planet."

"I will, Magistrate. Thank you."

Rivka hesitated. "What are you thanking me for?"

"The opportunity to learn that we didn't fail in the mediation and arbitration. There was much more going on than we understood. Everything you've done since arriving was beyond anything we contemplated as viable courses of action. You are extremely wise." Billi Jane bowed deeply.

Rivka smiled. "I'm extremely jaded, having seen the worst of the sentient creatures. When you figure out the bad thing they're doing, the rest falls into place. Very few are clean. Not the people we deal with. They are the worst of the worst. Think of them as the dregs of the morally bankrupt while treating them like royalty."

"Is that where the F-rockets come in handy?"

"Royalty that needs a reality check. I probably swear too much. Maybe?" Rivka looked for an answer from Billi Jane.

"Not my place to say that you are willing to swear at anybody and everybody for any slight, real or perceived."

Rivka's face fell. Billi Jane looked like a little girl. She smiled innocently. "Tell Cole not to take his eyes off these people. They're a bit unpredictable," Rivka said and closed the airlock hatch.

Rivka called down the corridor, "Clodagh! Fire up the engines and take us back to Tempran Silver. And tow that broken-down yacht."

"We'll have to release *Destiny's Vengeance*," Clodagh shouted back.

"*Vengeance* can fly itself, plus it gives us a little extra firepower to convince the riffraff to join us in heading back to the planet." Rivka hurried to the bridge.

Clodagh let her have the captain's seat since she knew she'd have to use the main comm.

"Give me a broadcast channel so I can talk to all the ships at the same time, please." Rivka settled into the chair and stared at the tactical view of the system. "And tell Ankh he can reactivate that Gate. No one is going anywhere."

"Broadcast is live, Magistrate." Clodagh pointed at her like a movie director calling for action.

"Attention, Tempran Silver refugees. You are on starships that have been illegally flown away from the planet. You are ordered to immediately return to Tempran Silver, where your status will be individually reviewed. The board of directors will issue new guidance regarding their status and the way ahead soon after we return all ships to the planet's surface, where you will disembark and return to your homes. I am not taking questions at this time. By order of Magistrate Rivka Anoa."

She closed the channel.

"You didn't want to tell them that non-compliance would see great harm befall them?"

"We'll threaten those who think they're too good to follow orders. Maybe send *Destiny's Vengeance* after them to give them the finger up close and personal. Have you let the ambassador know that we've had to decouple his ship?"

"Yes, Magistrate," Clevarious replied. "The ship is already being flown to the far point of the civilian armada so it can interdict anyone who runs for the Gate. Erasmus apologizes for the lie Ankh told earlier."

"Say what?" Rivka scowled at the overhead.

"They never shut the Gate down. They only placed a black image over it to make it appear that it was shut down. They found it easier to hack into each ship than to access the Gate itself."

Rivka bellowed, "I apologized to that stupid cat for no reason!"

"He is quite intelligent," Clevarious said softly. "Willful, arrogant, and confident that he is the most cat any cat could ever be, but not stupid."

"Thanks for that, C. I didn't realize that." Rivka waited for a moment. "Not. I made fun of Terry Henry Walton for calling that cat his arch-nemesis. I understand, and even more so since Wenceslaus now has minions to do his bidding. Wait a minute. He had minions on *War Axe*, too. That damn cat!"

Clodagh laughed and held up her hand. "Guilty as charged. He gets what he wants, and you don't even know that you've been played."

"That's right! It was you who sent him to *Peacekeeper*, my first ship."

"Not me." Clodagh held her hands up in surrender. As if to defend his human, yapping echoed down the corridor as Titan raced toward the bridge.

"And now Tiny Man Titan is getting in on the action."

The small dog-like creature bounced onto the bridge and yapped until Clodagh picked him up.

The tactical screen showed all ships complying with Rivka's order. They were slowly turning and lumbering toward Tempran Silver. "There's a problem we can avoid."

"You wouldn't have shot them down, would you?"

"No. I can't see capital punishment for an entire class of people, those who held themselves out as better than the other side. They're going to learn that they need the labor force more than Labor needs them. Who knows? We may get a new generation of people willing to get their hands dirty."

"We can hope," Clodagh agreed.

Rivka stood and gestured for her to take the captain's chair. "I'm going to check on Lewis."

She left the bridge and found Red standing to the side. "You been here the whole time?"

"We got bad guys surrounding us. I'm not letting you out of my sight."

Rivka couldn't fault his loyalty. "Works for me. Cargo bay." She strode briskly down the port corridor and through the small airlock. She found Tyler hovering over the empty Pod-doc. "Where's Lewis?"

"In his quarters, getting tended to by Kennedy. Or maybe that he's in her quarters getting tended to. Honestly, I'm at a loss. He's one hundred percent, before you ask."

"Then what is Kennedy tending to?" Rivka groaned at Tyler's look. "Never mind. He's earned a few minutes' respite. We're heading back to Tempran Silver and bringing the intransigent government with us."

"They abdicated, fled, or simply scoffed at the labor force. Is there a precedent for a government bailing on its people?"

"Yes, but not like this. It's like they'd been planning it forever. How do you load all your ships with your people without manifests and rosters? I didn't pick up on it because I hadn't contemplated such a thing. And since I'm talking, the timeline was too short following the mine collapse. They were planning it prior to that."

"Contingency plan triggered by the collapse?" Tyler offered.

"That's what I would say." She gave him a hug and left the cargo bay.

Rivka went to her quarters to catch up on paperwork.

She also wanted to look into the law that might apply regarding the government stealing the wealth of the planet. She was sure most governments did it, enriching their people, but not as brazenly. Was there a specific law or anything in Tempran Silver local statutes that required notice or some other public disclosure when spending from the treasury?

Red waited in the corridor.

"Send me Dennicron and Chaz. I have research I need them to do." Rivka closed the door.

CHAPTER SEVENTEEN

<u>Tempran Silver, Negotiations Tent</u>

Zagreb sauntered in, almost sashaying as he took in the cowed persona across the table. Galwyn stared at the table, wearing the same clothes from two days prior. He looked nearly homeless in his dishevelment.

"They left. The planet is ours," Zagreb declared, then spun the chair and sat on it backward, resting his crossed arms on the chair's back.

"It's not that easy. A change of government has a few more moving parts. The board of directors has reconsidered and will continue to govern the planet."

"They won't. They don't have our approval. Get them off the planet."

"We're back to civil war, then?" Rivka asked.

"They showed their mettle. What a pack of cowards."

"If you chase them away, they take Tempran Silver's entire wealth, including all the starships. And this time, I won't stop them."

"Thanks for that, but we're well ahead of you. Our mechanics are disabling the ships as we speak."

Rivka wanted to slap the smug expression off his face.

"And we're setting up tribunals. They'll be convicted of treason and turned loose in the streets without masks."

Rivka glared at him. "I'm not going to let that happen. They are the legitimate government, and we're here to forestall a civil war."

"There's nothing civil about what they tried to do to us. We're only turning it around. Fair play and all."

"And I just told you that you're not doing that."

"This is an internal Tempran Silver affair, Magistrate. As such, your services are no longer needed, and I invite you to leave."

"Sorry. You don't have the authority since the legitimate government is still in place. Nice try though, Zagreb."

The soldier fumed. "You'll want to leave the planet, Rivka. It's not safe for you to be here."

He threw his chair into the table as he lurched to his feet and stormed off.

Red was up and ready, but Rivka called him off.

"I never got to touch him, once again," Rivka grumbled.

"He has grown more aggressive," Red suggested.

"Maybe I can talk with him," Sahved offered, having joined them for the morning. Billi Jane and Tex were present too, along with Dennicron, Chaz, and Lindy. It was a full house with Galwyn and Zagreb, but Zagreb had left, and Galwyn was headed for the doorway.

"Galwyn," Rivka called. He stopped but didn't look back.

"They're worse than us," he replied.

"I'll talk to him. See what's going on." Rivka moved close to Galwyn, but he bolted as she neared.

She spoke, but he couldn't hear since he was already gone. "You were bad too. Maybe you're a little bit better now. What a shitshow."

Rivka flopped into the chair Zagreb had turned around.

"Red, what lines are closed and what lines are open?" She slouched and stared at the roof.

"Why am I the voice of betting?"

"Red..." Rivka let that linger.

"Fine. Closed, swearing, first blood, first arrest. There is some debate regarding first punch, but it'll probably be declared void and reopened. Open lines are first running, planet destroyed by Labor, planet destroyed by government, and case closed."

"Planet destroyed? What the hell?" Rivka leaned forward to check Red's expression.

He shrugged. "You made me the messenger, and now you want to shoot the messenger." He looked at Lindy for support. She stared back with a blank expression. "That's a steaming pile of bullshit."

"People are betting that this planet will be destroyed," Rivka reiterated. "Unbelievable."

"It's quite believable," Dennicron said. "Humanity's fascination with the morbid is as old as the species itself. Of course you remember the Jack the Ripper case. How bizarre yet gripping. Once it was made public, it became the talk of all the news channels for days! No one gets days' worth of coverage, but Jack the Ripper did. Horrific as that entity was." Dennicron glanced at Rivka. "Sorry. You were being rhetorical."

"Red, don't tell me the betting lines ever again." Rivka stood and put on her mask.

"Did you just *Kobayashi Maru* me? You'll ask, and I'm not supposed to tell you. Then you'll yell at me, and then you'll look into my mind. I'm going to give you an eyeful of naked me!"

Rivka stepped back to sympathize with Lindy for having to live with Red.

"No mercy," Lindy told her. "You asked for that."

"In a convoluted way, maybe I did. Back to the ship. We're going to see Zagreb in his office. I want to know what happened to Elbird and Pekrov, and I want to make it abundantly clear to Zagreb that he is *not* in charge of Tempran Silver. An illegal civil war will get him locked up."

"It'll also get a lot of people killed. I don't trust that guy won't light the sky on fire."

"I know you want to fight him, Red, but in this, I agree with you. He might just be unhinged enough to burn it all even with him inside so he can prove his point." Rivka held the door for everyone to head outside.

Red waited. "What does he need to prove?"

"That if he can't be in charge, no one can."

Tempran Silver, Labor Offices

Wyatt Earp arrived before Zagreb.

"The building looks closed," Clodagh said. "No one around. Minimal power." She brought up the infrared view. A closer inspection showed six people inside when there should have been hundreds of staff and out-of-work miners.

"Where's Zagreb?" Rivka asked.

No one answered.

"Clevarious, I know you have his vehicle tagged, or even him. Where is he? We have a warrant because two people disappear to open the top spot just when things turn interesting. Makes me wonder if he collapsed the mine too. Soldiers know how to blow stuff up."

"He's less than a kilometer away and should arrive in less than a minute," Clevarious confirmed.

"Thank you. Why were you holding out on me?"

"Ankh is still mad at you," Clevarious replied.

"What? He manipulated me with a lie so I would apologize to his cat!"

"Yes. It made him angry that you didn't just apologize in the first place. He loves Erasmus for his vibrant mind and Chrysanthemum for hers, but the only warm-blooded creature he loves is Wenceslaus. He tolerates everyone else, and you should probably be thankful for that."

"What about Ted?" Rivka replied. A dot appeared on the screen, showing the inbound vehicle with Zagreb on board.

"He is one with Ted intellectually, and they would be inseparable if it were not for Erasmus and Plato and, well, Ted's wife."

Rivka closed her eyes. "I'm sorry I asked. Tell Ankh I'm sorry, and I can't wait to hug him like a stuffed doll to express my joy at his existence."

"I don't know how to parse that information," Clevarious replied.

"Best not to." Rivka twirled her finger. "Shall we?"

She led the small parade to the airlock. She punched the big red button, but the outer door didn't open.

"Air's bad out there," Red reminded her.

She stepped inside, and Red and Lindy joined her. Red handed her a mask. She nodded in appreciation.

"What's going on, Magistrate? You don't seem to be yourself," he said. The airlock cycled, but Red blocked the button to open the outer door.

"Clevarious, turn off the audio pickup in here, please."

"Yes, Magistrate."

Rivka could only assume it was off. "It's us. All of us. I feel like I'm holding everyone back from being what they can be. Sahved is spinning in the wind. Dennicron is carrying around a broken Chaz. You guys have your little man, but you can't spend the time you need with him. I don't know the last time I saw Clodagh with Alanna. And that little fucking dog always barks at me."

Red laughed. "That is a steaming pile of excreted intestinal parasites. Are you going through menopause or something?"

Lindy balled a fist and punched him in the chest.

"Ow! I'm just asking a question."

Rivka shook her head. "Thanks, Lindy. I'm willing to punch him when necessary. It's not any of that stuff. I'm in perfect health, of course. The pilots and their boyfriends. The pilots raising the children. Animals running rampant."

"And we wouldn't have it any other way." Red flicked his fingers at her as if he were tossing something away. "You have this same conversation with yourself about once a month. We wouldn't be here if we didn't want to be.

Although you won't let me punch Zagreb in the face, you give me a purpose, and Lindy has given me a life.

"Even Ankh! I'm proud of the little guy. He spoofed you to get you to apologize to his cat! I didn't laugh as much when I heard that as I am now because that could be the funniest thing I've *ever* heard. A Crenellian, lying not for personal gain but for a cat who is a total asshole."

Rivka smiled. "An asshole he is proud of and shows to everyone, whether they want to see it or not."

"The most cat any cat could ever cat," Lindy added.

"I love you guys," Rivka stated. "Now, let's go see Zagreb. Maybe you'll get your wish, and he'll resist our efforts to question him."

"Are you going to arrest him?" Red asked hopefully.

"I have probable cause to search, but not enough to arrest him. I'll keep looking because he's at the heart of all the bad shit that's going on."

"Are you ready to face the world, Magistrate?" Red asked, hand hovering over the button.

"I'm always ready, but sometimes more than others. Right now, it's the former."

Red looked at Lindy. "Does that mean we're ready to go?"

Lindy nodded, then shook her head.

"Damn women in my life can't talk straight. Nice! It never means nice. 'Good enough' is a put-down. Don't pee standing up!"

"Red, will you push the button, please?" Rivka tipped her chin at the panel near the outer hatch.

He hammered the button with his fist and forced his way in front of Rivka to be first out of the hatch. Rivka and

Lindy followed him out. The hatch closed as the next group prepared to cycle through.

"They'll catch up," Rivka said.

Red hurried to stay in front of her.

They went through the front door, then helped themselves to the second level and straight on to the labor leader's office. Zagreb was inside but had not yet sat down. He saw Rivka coming and rolled his eyes. He headed for the rear door.

"Hold up, Zagreb. I have a few questions."

"Fuck your questions." He passed through the door and slammed it behind him.

"Red, you're up. If you have to hit him, so be it."

Red ran full speed and hit the door for all he was worth. He bounced back, staggered, and fell.

Lindy jumped to his side to lift him. He stood, groggy.

"It was like running into a solid bulkhead."

"Railgun," Rivka advised.

Lindy raised hers and fired where she thought the locking mechanism would be. Then she stitched a series near the top of the door and then the bottom. She kicked it, and it still held.

She blasted it twice more before it sagged on its hinges. Red kicked it in and stepped through the opening.

Dennicron was the first to arrive, having sprinted through the building. Then came Sahved, Billi Jane, and Tex.

"What were you shooting at?" Dennicron asked.

"The door. Zagreb made a run for it."

"Dennicron, with me," Red said. He jogged through a

narrow corridor to steps leading down. He slowed going down the stairs.

Rivka followed ten paces behind, with Lindy attached to her hip. Sahved lumbered along, ducking in the low-ceilinged corridor.

Billi Jane ran ahead. She was the only one who looked normal in the confined space.

"What was this built for? It's probably not up to code. A secret corridor to a secret dungeon," Rivka quipped. "Carry on."

"Would you keep it down?" Red whispered harshly.

Rivka threw her hands up and tried to look innocent. "Zagreb is more of a threat to himself than he is to us."

"He was a soldier. He'll have some tricks up his sleeve. Now, let me do my job."

Red crouched, keeping his railgun at the ready. "Dennicron," he whispered. "Sensors?"

"Movement up ahead. One person. Go!"

Red ran, fired by the thought of closing with Zagreb for a hand-to-hand session. He vibrated at the opportunity, abandoning all pretense of stealth. "Come on, Zagreb. Don't be a coward. The more you run, the more tired you'll be when I beat your ass!"

"Didn't he tell me to be quiet?" Rivka muttered, falling farther behind. "Did you really tell him no stand-up peeing?"

"He makes a mess. Then I have to yell at him to clean it up. It's not pretty. Now Dery is trying to do it while flying."

Rivka grunted deep in her throat as she tried to stifle a laugh. "What would I do without you guys?"

"Be bored out of your mind?" Lindy suggested. "We better hurry."

"No running. I'll keep that line open to the end." They stepped up their pace but didn't resort to running. They left that to Red and Dennicron.

"Exiting," Dennicron called.

"Dammit!" Red sprinted toward the door. He reached it and got it slammed in his face. He recoiled but had blocked most of it with his railgun. "Zagreb, I'm coming for you."

"Oh, it's you? I thought it was the government looking to arrest me. They do that, you know."

The door opened casually. Zagreb stood in the open air, struggling to get his mask on.

Red waited. He'd never taken his mask off. Dennicron circled around to block Zagreb's exit.

With the mask in place and breathing normally, Zagreb tried to look casual. "What's up, Red? You look winded."

Red wasn't breathing hard. "I think I'll punch you in the head just because you are a total jag off."

Zagreb angled his body to limit his exposure to the inevitable attack and raised his fists.

"Stop," Rivka said from behind them.

Red had his railgun slung over his back. His shoulders slumped. "Magistrate, your timing couldn't have been worse. I was ready to deliver the hammer fist."

"Zagreb is only a suspect, not a perp," Rivka explained. She swirled past her bodyguard. Dennicron blocked the man from backing away. She grabbed his arm. "What happened to Elbird?"

Dead and tossed into a pit. "Nothing. He was sick and took a leave of absence."

"Interesting. What about Pekrov?"

Soldiers took him away. He was supposed to be killed as well. "Too much stress. He also took a leave of absence."

"You killed them both. Red, if you'd secure the prisoner, I'd appreciate it." Rivka gave him room.

"With pleasure." Red stepped forward.

Zagreb was fast and well-practiced. He lashed out with a leg sweep that nearly took Red off his feet, but he crouched and blocked the worst of it. Red changed his target and swung from the ground up to deliver as much power as he had into Zagreb's groin.

The man came off the ground and collapsed on top of Red with a grunt and a groan. Red pushed him away and straightened. Red stepped on his hand as he walked away. "One punch. Sheesh. We need tougher perps, Magistrate."

"He's a bad one." Rivka took his arm. "What were you planning with the planet?"

Ignite the atmosphere. There were only four hours remaining. Others placed the device. He didn't know where it was.

Rivka jumped back. "He's the one who's going to torch the sky. Him and the other soldiers who joined the labor group. That's why there's nobody here. They're going to do what I thought the government was doing, leave the planet and blow it up in their wake." She turned back to Zagreb. "That's insane. You have to stop it."

"That starship has left the space station, Rivka," Zagreb grunted. He tried to stand but could only make it to his knees. He bent in half with one hand on the ground.

"Crap," Rivka complained. "We better notify the government. Evacuate as many as they can from both sides."

Dennicron used her comm chip to relay the message using the ship's equipment.

"The government is less than amused, but they'll give the order. Their people will return to the ships."

Rivka blew out a breath. "Which are already being filled with other people. That means space will be at a premium. It could get ugly." Rivka pointed at the ship. "I need to talk with Grainger."

She groaned, then ran around the building to where *Wyatt Earp* was parked at the side of the front lot.

Lindy ran after her. Red all but dragged Zagreb. The others stayed with him. Sahved started peppering Zagreb with questions, none of which he answered.

Through the airlock and down the corridor, Rivka burst into her quarters and brought up the hologrid. "Grainger, we have roughly four hours before the labor leader becomes the lead terrorist and tries to kill everyone in this city."

Grainger scowled. "I hoped it wouldn't come to that. I thought you could stop them."

"Me too, Grainger. I didn't believe they were serious until I did, and then it was too late. They were cagey about it, hiding their intent, and the labor guy, Zagreb, killed the other two negotiators, who didn't have a clue. Their deaths were instrumental to his plan for taking over. He'll be in our brig momentarily, along with Wristler, the government guy who did everything he could to plunder the treasury."

Grainger leaned forward and spoke clearly. "Is there anyone worth saving on that planet?"

"All of them. Only the few at the top are criminals and assholes. The average worker is just fine. The people are never the problem, Grainger. It's always the government. Power corrupts. You know the deal, especially now that you're in charge."

"Hey! I'm in charge of being personally responsible for you lot. It's not a job anyone envies."

Rivka nodded with a brief smile. "Four hours, Grainger. We're not going to be able to get everyone off."

"Make sure you and your team evacuate. Don't make yourself a martyr," Grainger warned.

"I've got work to do," Rivka replied and signed off.

CHAPTER EIGHTEEN

<u>Tempran Silver, Spaceport</u>

"This is no surprise," Rivka muttered, looking at the enhanced view on *Wyatt Earp's* main screen. "It's a dog's breakfast down there."

"Is not. Titan eats much better than that," Clodagh countered.

Chaos reigned. People mobbed the ships' access hatches, way more than could fit aboard the ships. "If we land, we'll get swamped under a human tidal wave."

"I recommend we remain cloaked and shielded."

"The only way to stop this madness is to find the soldiers and their pyrotechnics," Rivka said. "Ankh, can you come to the bridge? I have science questions that could take a great deal of compute power."

"Are you going to vent your spleen because I might have misled you?" Ankh asked, using the speakers instead of his preferred method of the internal comm chip.

"I have forgiven you, the cat, the ship, and the entire universe for your transgressions."

"I doubt it," Ankh replied.

"I need info, and we don't have time to fuck around. Can a device ignite the sky? Where would they have to put it, and then how much damage will it do? I already know the answer to the first question is yes. What about the other two?"

"See? I didn't need to come to the bridge at all. Honestly, Magistrate, you would save so much time if you didn't insist on having your nonsensical meetings."

"Don't make me come back there," Rivka replied. "Please, Ankh. I need those answers, priority to optimal location to place a device."

"We'll look into it, but we need to collect more data, like pollutant particle density and purity."

"Work with Clevarious to fly wherever you need to, but please be quick about it. I'll apologize to the cat again if you want."

A click indicated that he'd cut off his microphone.

"Too much?" Rivka asked.

Clodagh shook her head. "I'm sure he appreciated your gesture."

"The fact that you could say such nonsense with a straight face makes me wonder how often you lie and get away with it."

"Not ever." Clodagh nodded emphatically.

"Come closer so I can touch you." Rivka held out her hand in the zombie maneuver she used with the crew.

"Sorry, Magistrate. I just got super busy. Ship is accelerating away. Collection ducts are porting. Analysis is underway."

Rivka watched the screen as they raced over the city.

She could barely see anything except the tops of the tallest buildings. The ship accelerated in a straight line until the air cleared, then it turned on its wing and flew back on a parallel course. *Wyatt Earp* was traveling at three times the speed of sound. The sonic boom probably scared the hell out of the people on the ground.

They had to be thinking it was the end of days. Terrorists preparing to destroy the planet and everyone remaining on its surface.

"What if we used the ships to shuttle people to the resort where the air is clear? The pollution is relatively localized. Relatively," Rivka posited.

"The city is in a bowl without wind. Getting the people outside of it would save them, and it's probably the most expeditious," Clodagh agreed.

Rivka accessed the comm and called the ship's pilots. "You don't have to go to space. You only have to move the people to where the air is clear."

"We can get to orbit, or we can shuttle people outside the city. We can't do both," one pilot responded.

"Are you that low on fuel?"

"We already left the planet once and returned. We weren't prepared for two such flights."

"Refuel!" Rivka blurted the common-sense answer.

"We took all there was for the first trip," the pilot responded. "It's a one-way trip, Magistrate, and we're going to space."

Rivka scowled. "So much for the good idea. They don't want to stay on the planet; simple as that. The pilots are now in charge, a third contender for primacy. It's absolute madness. Brings us back to what we really need to do, and that's find the perps and disable the device. That is now Priority One."

Despite their speed, they took forty minutes to complete the aerial survey since it wasn't just back and forth over the city. It was at various altitudes, too. The patchwork flight resulted in a three-dimensional model of the pollutant cloud.

"We'd been led to believe it was the end of all things if that cloud ignited. What will the yield be if it blows?" Rivka asked.

"Still calculating, Magistrate," Clevarious replied.

"Optimal ignition point?"

"Still calculating." Clevarious spoke in a monotone. Rivka found that upsetting. She was agitated and wanted answers she wasn't getting. They had less than three hours before the explosion if Zagreb's information was still valid. The soldiers could have changed their plan after both sides attempted to escape.

"What if they did something to the ships?" Rivka wondered. "The labor team had access to all the ships. They were supposedly disabling them to prevent the government from taking them.

"Your first conspiracy theory was wrong, thinking the government was going scorched earth. Now I think you're onto something," Red suggested, leaning through the bridge hatch. The sound of wings beating confirmed that Dery was nearby. "I guess you weren't completely wrong or even mostly wrong. You just fingered the wrong perps."

"I knew there was a conspiracy somewhere. I could feel it in my bones, but I never saw it in anyone's mind. That would have made it much easier, but we can't lament the past. We have to deal with the present to secure our future."

"Sounds like a political speech," Red said. "But apropos."

"When did you start using words like 'apropos?'"

"Magistrate," Clevarious interrupted. "Optimal ignition point is center mass, directly over the opening to the underground mine. Destruction of the city will be nearly total. A fuel-air explosive relies on concussive force and overpressure to do the damage."

"What can we do to limit the concussion?"

"Limit the overpressure? I'm not sure it can be done. I'll submit the question to the Singularity. I'll share the answer as soon as we have it."

Rivka nodded. "Center mass. That means the detonator has to be airborne, either a drone or a rocket launched into the atmosphere. Where are the optimal launch points?"

"For a drone, anywhere, but for a rocket, directly below as that gives a no-wind trajectory two chances to detonate at the right point."

Rivka studied the screen. The best launch point appeared as a small icon. "What kind of payload will the rocket have to carry?"

"Not much in the way of fuel, but the detonator will have to be substantial. Temperature needs to be north of two thousand degrees Celsius across a broad area. It's not simply burning magnesium, but a massive amount of magnesium to create the conditions for a self-perpetuating fire."

"We're not talking throwing magnesium strips in water, are we?" Rivka offered.

"No," Clevarious replied. "It'll be more involved. Orders

of magnitude greater. Payload of five hundred kilograms, at least, and there's no way they developed this over the last day. It would take months for your average humans on Tempran Silver to build this device. They've been planning it long before they threatened the government with civil war. I'm surprised the board of directors didn't get wind of the plan."

"The board of directors had their heads buried. I'm not sure they cared to look. They gave orders. They weren't into subterfuge, only intimidation and coercion. Okay, let's go looking for a delivery system—a rocket that can handle a five-hundred-kilogram payload. We'll discount drones or any engines dependent upon air, unlike the starships, which use drives that don't generate heat in the thousands of degrees. There aren't a lot of options for the bad guys."

"There has to be someone who knows where these soldiers are. There *has* to be," Red insisted.

"But who? We can barely see while we're walking around down there. We wouldn't know who to roust. I can't just touch everyone, and the people evacuating won't be the ones who are part of the inner circle."

"Luxury yacht," Red suggested. "The inner circles take care of themselves."

"Clevarious, drop us right on top of them. We'll jump down and board the yacht. I'll *talk* to everyone on that ship."

"On our way, Magistrate," Clevarious confirmed.

Clodagh gave a thumbs-up from the navigation console. Ryleigh was flying the ship. Kennedy was with Lewis until Rivka declared him fit for duty. Aurora was off-duty, which meant she was watching Alanna.

The children. "Dery, can you help us?" Rivka asked.

Dery flew past his parents to Rivka. He settled on her arm. She hugged him to her shoulder with her other arm.

"Please?" she pleaded.

Life is fleeting.

"That's ominous. Are you telling me that we won't figure this out in time?"

Life will go on, Dery replied.

"I love you, little man," Rivka said. "I have no idea what you're telling me, but I feel better for it." She faced the main screen. "Drop me, Red, Sahved, Dennicron, Chaz, Tex, and Billi Jane at the *Tempran Minerals*. The rest of you, find that launch platform and a way to stop them from sending that payload into the sky."

"You heard the Magistrate!" Red bellowed down the corridor. "Saddle up!"

He ran for the airlock.

Rivka jogged after him. Red handed her a mask, then put on his. None of the others needed a mask, which was why Rivka had chosen them.

Rivka, Red, Dennicron, and Sahved were first into the airlock. It cycled, and the outer hatch popped. *Wyatt Earp* was hovering nearly ten meters above the mist-covered ground. "Are you going to be okay, Sahved?" Rivka asked. At his look, she knew the answer. "You stay. Help them find the device."

Red vaulted out the door and disappeared. Rivka went after him. Dennicron stepped through, and Sahved punched the button to cycle the airlock for the next group.

Red stepped away from where he impacted, limping with the first two steps before he straightened.

Rivka grunted on impact. She took a couple moments before standing upright. "How about those nanos?"

Dennicron slammed hard into the deck. The SCAMPs weighed hundreds of kilograms, but they were the equivalent of a human-sized dump truck in durability.

Didn't feel a thing, Chaz told them.

"Me either, dear," Dennicron added.

Red and Rivka headed for the luxury yacht's crowded ramp. They recognized some of the faces from the last time they were on board.

"There's plenty of time," Rivka called.

"Gangway! Magistrate is coming through," Red shouted, but the bodies packed tighter toward the hatch.

"People!" Rivka waved to get their attention. No one was boarding. There was something holding them back at the hatch. They turned while making sure no one took their spots in line. "We are looking for the device that Zagreb and his people intend to use to ignite the atmosphere. That means interrogating every single person on this ship. I can expedite that, and it will only take a few minutes, but you have to let me pass."

"Bullshit, we do! You just try to keep me off this ship," someone grumbled from up the ramp. They packed themselves in even tighter.

Red reached out to drag the nearest person away, but Rivka stopped him. "That will be a fight we can't win. These people are terrified. We have to find another way."

"Can you touch their legs?" Dennicron suggested and pointed at the tarmac beneath the open ramp.

"That I can. Red, I'll need to sit on your shoulders for those at the top of the ramp."

"Say what?" Red looked sideways at her.

Rivka motioned for him to take a knee. She climbed onto his shoulders, and he stood. "Don't you wish I was a little bigger?" he asked.

"You're just fine. You're not winning this one, Red. Take me to the front, please."

Red moved to where the ramp entered the ship.

"Where's the device?" Rivka shouted and bounced her hand from ankle to ankle. The thoughts were jumbled. People weren't listening.

Dennicron, I'll need you to deliver a voice that echoes off the ship. Loud as you can.

Dennicron cupped her hands around her mouth and turned the volume to eleven. "Where's the device?"

Rivka almost fell off Red's shoulders, so he clamped down on her thighs to hold her in place. The group on the ramp stopped jostling. She retraced her efforts from ankle to ankle. Red moved quickly down the ramp until Rivka was up too high.

She jumped down.

"Once more, Dennicron, and I'll get the rest."

A second iteration delivered the same result. The sheer volume of Dennicron's question rocked their world. Rivka darted her hand in and out of the group, listening to their minds as fast as she could.

She reached the bottom of the ramp, straightened, and nearly fell over.

"You okay?" Red asked, pulling her to him and holding her tightly. "Anything in their minds?"

"Not in this group. They must be already on the ship." Her chin fell to her chest. "We better hurry."

Red didn't move. "Not if you can't stand."

Rivka pushed away. "I can stand. Just need to catch my breath." She lifted a hand to her temple and held it there as if it would help the headache go away. So many thoughts, disparate, jumbled, punctuated by the fear of a horrible death. The people on the ramp saw themselves as victims. They might have been more involved, but she would not learn that via the rapid-fire engagement.

Priorities dictated that everything else could wait. If she couldn't find the device, people would assuredly die. Their terror was not unfounded, but it was exhausting.

"I'll be fine. Dennicron and the others can force the people away from the hatch. I need to get inside. This isn't negotiable, even if we start a riot."

Dennicron, Tex, and Billi Jane nodded as one.

Red aimed his railgun in the air, dialed it to automatic, and unleashed a short burst. That drew everyone's attention.

Dennicron jumped five meters into the air and landed on the rail by the hatch. She levered herself into the space and pushed the nearest people back, but there was nowhere for them to go. A bone snapped, and the sound was worse than a rifle shot.

"That's it. We're done playing!" Red roared. He waded into the line on the ramp and bodily threw people to the tarmac. He plucked them off one at a time until they realized the man was going to throw them over the rail if they didn't get out of the way. He laughed maniacally, then fired again.

The rest ran, leaving Dennicron and the injured individual at the front, facing two soldiers with a see-through screen blocking the way into the ship.

Rivka strolled up the ramp. "Thanks, Red. Tex, get this one to the Pod-doc. Coordinate directly with the ship."

"Yes, ma'am," Tex drawled. He carefully lifted the injured person and loped away.

Rivka put him out of her mind. She had more work to do.

"The mean soldiers aren't going to let us in," Red said with a smile. "Can I kill them?"

"If we push on the screen, they might push back." Rivka winked at Red.

"I hear you." He waited for her to get close.

Rivka squeezed between Red and Dennicron, who pushed on the screen. Dennicron maxed her servos, and Red grunted with the effort. One of the guards put his hands on the screen and leaned into it. Rivka touched where his hands were. It wasn't like physically touching him, but it gave her a connection. "Where's the device?"

Four soldiers. In the city. He didn't know more than that.

"Now we're getting somewhere," Rivka said softly. She stepped back and flopped down.

"Screw this," Red growled. He aimed at the four attachment points and fired, punching holes in the top of the screen. He reared back and kicked. Dennicron followed by pushing the top down on the two soldiers. They attempted to pull their sidearms, but it was too late. They were trapped under the screen.

Rivka walked over the top of them. On the other side, she bent and rested a hand on each of their heads. "How are they going to detonate the atmosphere?"

An air balloon somewhere in the city with a drone to drive it.

Rivka laughed and used her comm chip to inform the ship. *They're going to use an air balloon and a drone, so they don't need to launch it directly beneath the optimal detonation point. Take out that balloon, please.*

Rivka relaxed.

"Anyone we need to roust?" Red asked, sounding disappointed.

"Let's see who's on this ship. Maybe we'll find Zagreb's insiders."

"I think his insiders are the ones launching that balloon. That means they have to have a way onto this ship, or they have another ship. I don't get the sense that his people are martyr types." Red remembered the ship from the last time he was on board. "The common room?"

"Let's see who's on board." Rivka followed Red to the access with the marks from her combat team working the door. She attempted to open it, but Red pushed her out of the way.

"Don't be a nutcase. I go first." Red stepped in and scanned the small crowd before he allowed Rivka to enter.

"Howdy, folks!" Rivka called. "How's it shaking?"

She looked for familiar faces but didn't see any.

"The board of directors isn't here," Red stated.

"I thought they'd be here," Rivka replied. "I'm surprised that they are not." She turned to the crowd of unfamiliar faces. "Who are you people?"

They grumbled, but no one answered.

Rivka strolled into the group. There was nowhere they could go to get away from her. "Who are you?" she touched them as she sashayed by.

Labor leaders. Zagreb's friends. No one from the hands-on mining community. No one from the government-corporate side.

"Time to go, Red." Rivka headed for the hatch.

At the airlock, they found the two guards still trapped under the clear screen. The people outside were working their way toward the opening.

Rivka held up one hand, and they stopped despite their fear. "Let me off, and then it's all yours."

She strolled down the ramp, and at the halfway point, she jumped over the rail to the tarmac. Red jumped over too. Dennicron stayed on the ramp, and the people cleared out of her way. Once she was by, the passengers raced to get on board.

Rivka watched for a moment. The panic was followed by relief on their faces as they found a seat on a ship leaving Tempran Silver.

"Are we going to just let them go?" Red asked. The others huddled near them watched Rivka intently.

"Yes. We're going to let the yacht and whoever is on it go. I don't think finding that balloon is going to be easy. Visibility sucks, and our sensors aren't working like they should. If we don't see the balloon, we could be caught in the explosion unless we abandon the planet."

Dennicron offered, "I believe we might be able to dampen the explosion. This is one of the tasks you asked of the Singularity. We need to find thirty to forty tons of quicklime, and we can possibly break the detonation chain."

"Where are we going to find that much quicklime?"

"It's not currently on the planet."

"Can we produce it?" Rivka asked.

"No."

"Do you have any plans that we can actually implement?"

"We're still studying what is possible."

"We're nearly out of time, Dennicron. A perfect plan *later* is of no use to us. A good enough plan *now* is what we need." Rivka gritted her teeth. "Billi Jane, find us ground transport. We'll look for the balloon from ground level. I think we're going to see it, or at least where it can be. It has to be pretty big to haul a minimum of five hundred kilograms."

"Be right back," Billi Jane said and ran into the ever-present murk that passed for the air on Tempran Silver.

Less than a minute later, Billi Jane drove up in a limousine.

"Abandoned vehicles are everywhere," she explained. "With the keys inside."

They loaded up, leaving Billi Jane behind the wheel. "I don't know where Tex went, but if he hasn't boarded the ship yet, have him meet us."

"I feel bad about that," Dennicron said. "Humans aren't as hard as they should be."

"It was a mob, and there's nothing you can do to influence it except what Red did. Dismantle it one person at a time."

"He's at the edge of the spaceport. We'll pick them up on our way out," Billi Jane explained.

Despite her small size, her driving was adept, the product of upgraded subroutines shared by Chaz and Dennicron.

Red looked miserable. "There's a kid driving."

Rivka laughed. "What's the worst thing that can happen?"

The limousine slammed into a vehicle racing from the other direction. Two bodies ejected through the other's windshield and bounced off the limousine on their way to the ground, where they lay still. Steam rose from the mangled combustion engine. Other engines growled in the distance as the last to evacuate rushed toward the ships.

Red groaned, cracked his neck, and looked for a way out of the vehicle. The doors were twisted enough to resist his efforts to open them. He hammered out a window using the butt of his railgun, scraped the glass away, and crawled out.

He reached inside. "Magistrate."

She took his hand, and he pulled her to safety. One by one, the others climbed out. "Are you okay?" Red asked.

"I feel like I've been in a car accident, but besides that, I'm fine. How about you?"

"I admit that being any bigger would have precluded my exodus from the vehicle. I am good with my current size."

"Why are you talking like that?" Rivka asked, checking the SCAMPs. They were fine, not a single scratch.

"Lindy likes 'em big and nerdy. I'm giving her a treat."

"I should have figured it came down to sex."

"Are you surprised?" Red shrugged and snorted.

Rivka stretched and turned serious. "We better find another vehicle. There's a balloon out there ready to go skyward. We cannot allow it."

Red checked the direction with Dennicron and jogged

away. They followed in a line, with the Magistrate running alongside Dennicron and Chaz. Billi Jane brought up the rear, her short legs moving twice as fast to keep pace. It would have been comical had the stakes not been so high.

It would be the end of everyone left behind.

CHAPTER NINETEEN

<u>**_Wyatt Earp_, above the City**</u>

"This is making me angry," Clodagh complained. "The sensors are useless. Nothing but ghosts and echoes. Clevarious, there has to be something you can do."

"We are working on decluttering the interference by inverting the polarity through a multi-band oscillation optimized by drivelation…"

"Just stop," Clodagh begged. "You're saying nonsense words. There's nothing you can do, is there?"

"No. Proximity appears to be the most effective. Recommend we increase speed, spiraling in and out of the target area."

"Recommend altitude of one hundred and seventy-five meters," Clodagh said.

Ryleigh replied, "Ten meters above the highest object in the area. That's cutting it a little close."

"We need to see the balloon as it's inflating. I'd go lower if we could."

"One-seven-five meters AGL," Ryleigh confirmed.

The ship accelerated in a constant bank. Despite the antigravity plates, they could feel the strain.

Clodagh accessed the intercom. "All hands, brace yourselves for some erratic maneuvers. Cole, get the combat team ready to deploy, fully armored and armed."

Wings rhythmically flapped, slapping the deck with equal regularity. Clodagh forced herself out of the captain's seat to find Dery struggling down the corridor. The young boy smiled and shrugged.

Clodagh picked him up and carried him onto the bridge, then resumed her role as the ship's captain.

"I'm detecting a concentration of particles in our wake," Clevarious said.

"What does that mean?" Clodagh wondered.

"Where densities are changed, that means with an increase in one area, there is a commensurate decrease in another. There is a set number of particles."

"A firebreak," Clodagh suggested. "If we can stop the cascade, the atmosphere doesn't get torched."

"That is a supposition."

"Which means you aren't sure if the lesser density will be enough to stymy ignition."

"We're not sure," Clevarious admitted.

"It was a good plan while it lasted. We need to come up with something else, especially since we don't have thirty tons of quicklime, as Dennicron calculated. What else can interfere with the ignition?"

"Not allowing the device to explode at altitude," Clevarious replied.

Clodagh shook her head.

Cole interjected, "Bad Company squad is ready to

deploy. Send us down to search from below. We can cover a lot of ground down there. No one can hide a big-ass balloon, Clodagh. Let us go down there."

"What if we can't recover you before the device blows?"

"We'll find shelter in the open. No one will be better prepared to weather the explosion and concussion than us. We'll be fine."

"I'm not sure about that," Clodagh replied. "But you're right. We need to cover more ground. Faster isn't the solution I was looking for. We can't see jack while flying this fast. C, slow us down. Find a good spot to deploy the squad."

The ship slowed and drifted for a few seconds, then stopped.

"Already?"

"Ground Zero, as calculated. If they work their way outward from here, they should run into it."

"Deploy, gentlemen. We're at Ground Zero. Work your way outward, and good luck."

The cargo ramp opened. Clodagh brought up the live view beneath the heavy frigate so she could watch them drop. It was a long way, nearly two hundred meters, but they had jets, unlike the Magistrate and her team, who had jumped ten meters without any way to slow down.

"Continue our pattern, slower this time. Take us to a point one kilometer from here and then circle. We'll continue away from the center. Let the ground pounders cover from here to there."

Wyatt Earp moved away before the warriors hit the ground. The ship reached the designated distance and turned hard before accelerating along an arc one kilometer from the optimal detonation point. They stared at the live view in front of and below them. Clevarious kept the sensors at full strength to look through the clouds and the murk in the space between.

"Show us where you are," Clodagh pleaded.

We have a vehicle and are looking from this side, Rivka reported via her comm chip. The signal was clear, which meant she was close.

Cole and the warriors are down there too in their combat armor. Best to coordinate with them directly so you don't duplicate effort, Clodagh replied.

Rivka acknowledged that and signed off.

Clodagh hugged Dery to her while the search continued. "Do you sense anything?"

Everything, the boy replied mysteriously and without elaboration.

"You can fly now, Dery. We're not doing anything erratic." She held the boy out. His wings unfolded from his back and slowly beat the air. They sped up, and he lifted off his feet. He smiled and waved.

"If we were all so happy, life would be good."

Whee! Floyd shouted as she scrabbled to a stop. Her nails scraped the deck as she turned around and ran the other way, with Dery chasing her.

Tiny Man Titan barked from the other end of the corridor, but it was his happy, playful bark.

"Is no one afraid?" Clodagh wondered aloud.

Ryleigh turned to face her. "We're afraid for the people of Tempran Silver. We're afraid for our people who are down there when the locals have to be panicking. But life goes on. Being miserable while we're doing everything we can, all of it after we were invited to leave multiple times, won't help anyone.

"And no, I don't think we should have left when we had the chance. These people need help. Not the ones in power, but the average Joe, people like me and Furny. We're the ones you're looking to help."

Clodagh nodded. It was all about perspective. Children played. Workers worked. And the leadership worried. It was the way of things. Clodagh knew the Magistrate was worried. She could hear it in her voice.

"Now is the time to find that balloon," Clodagh said, but her wishes and desires didn't deliver the device to her. They continued to circle, heading outward with each pass while the crew watched the endless view of blurred buildings and nothing else.

The van moved at an infuriatingly slow speed. Rivka grumbled while Billi Jane maneuvered in and out of the debris on the road, along with dodging errant and random vehicles. They were the only ones driving away from the spaceport.

"Maybe we can stop some people and ask," Red suggested.

"Who?" Rivka wondered, pointing in various directions.

"The next person we see." Rivka gestured at a woman running on the sidewalk.

Billi Jane stopped and backed up to get in front of the woman. Red popped the door and hopped out, dodging to intercept the runner.

Rivka ducked out and held out her hands to get the woman to stop her frantic movements.

"Please!"

"Have you seen an air balloon or any soldiers?" Rivka asked and grabbed the woman's hands.

Nothing except panic.

"Get inside," Rivka told her as she released her arm.

"Nothing," Red guessed.

Rivka nodded. "Let's go. All we can do is try. What's the time?"

"Sixty-five minutes," Red replied.

"Shit." Rivka climbed back into the van. Red squeezed in, and Billi Jane sped off before the door was closed.

"Looking for a balloon. How fucking hard can it be?" Rivka shouted.

"When you can't see farther than ten meters in front of your face? Really fucking hard," Red shouted back.

Rivka shook her head. "Truth bomb delivered at hypersonic speed. We can't let the bad guys win."

"Nobody is letting them win. We're down here until the last minute. Keep in mind that we can Gate out of the atmosphere. All we need to do is get on board the ship prior to the device going off."

"Four hours wasn't an exact number. In Zagreb's mind, it was *about* four hours. How much time remains is a ballpark figure at best."

"That is some real fucking shit," Red grumbled, then perked up. "There!"

Faces in a window. Billi Jane nearly drove into the building but screeched to a stop on the sidewalk just short of the door. The injured woman cried out, ending with a whimper. Tex tried to comfort her.

Red and Rivka climbed out and rushed inside.

"Wait!" a man called, holding his hands out. "We decided not to go. Please don't take us."

Rivka shook her head. "We're not here to take you anywhere. We're looking for a balloon or soldiers moving a large device the size of a big crate." She took the man by the arm and listened intently.

Soldiers hurried by two hours earlier, heading toward the center of town.

Ground Zero. "We're going the wrong way. We need to go back."

"It's only a couple hundred meters. We haven't come far," Red protested.

"Time's wasting." Rivka shook the man's hand. "That's all I needed. Thank you."

They ran outside and climbed into the van. It was closer than they remembered. The door was still open. Rivke entered first. "Go back. They're that way." Rivka pointed toward the location they'd called Ground Zero. "The soldiers went that way."

There's a really tall building there, Chaz suggested. *We can't see the top of it from the ground. I suggest you climb to the roof, and from there,* Wyatt Earp *can pick us up.*

"Worried for your life, Chaz? Overpressure isn't going to hurt a SCAMP."

You get me wrong, Magistrate. I'm looking out for you.

"I'm not leaving until we end the threat to everyone who is trapped here."

Red gritted his teeth. "We need to leave before then,

Magistrate. We can't wait until the last minute."

The van bounced and twisted on the short drive to the high-rise. The group left the van as it was, keys inside. Tex walked with the injured woman, supporting her. The others entered the high-rise and looked for the stairs. They found them next to the elevators.

"Elevator," Red said, nodding at the woman in their charge.

Rivka pointed at Dennicron and Billi Jane. "You guys take the stairs. We'll take the elevator."

Dennicron and Billi Jane opened the door and pounded upward. Their footsteps faded while Rivka and her team waited for their ride. The elevator car was much smaller than expected.

"I'll walk," Rivka said.

"Not by yourself." Red snarled. "What a fucking goat rope. We'll meet you upstairs, Tex." Red and Rivka backed out of the elevator.

Rivka went first, taking the stairs two at a time. Her nano-enhanced physiology meant she was stronger and faster and had far greater endurance than an average human. Red was more enhanced, plus he worked out every chance he got. The run up thirty flights was barely more than an easy workout. They didn't catch up with Billi Jane and Dennicron.

On the top floor, they found the SCAMPs in the hall-way, studying another door that was locked and doubly secured. They were trying futilely to break it down.

Red looked at it for a moment, then brought his railgun to bear. Dennicron and Billi Jane dove out of the way.

Top of the highest building, Rivka transmitted to *Wyatt*

Earp. We're almost there now. Just need to break through this door.

On our way, Magistrate.

Red fired into the door, and the rounds ricocheted down the hall. He stopped after the first burst. "Never seen that before. Everyone stand back." Instead of the door, he aimed at the wall and stitched a line around the frame. He fired, waited, fired, and waited again. He connected the dots around the frame before slinging his railgun on his back.

Dennicron stopped him from pulling the frame out.

"In case they're waiting on the other side. I'll pull it out. You prepare to kill them."

Dennicron hadn't minced words. That was exactly what needed to happen. "Sounds like a good plan." Red cleared his line of fire.

Dennicron and Billi Jane used the power in their bodies to leverage the massive metal barrier. Tex jumped in to help. After a final surge, steps appeared beyond the gaping hole in the wall.

Red rushed in and up. Rivka bolted through the opening, carrying her neutron pulse weapon dialed to seven. She wasn't fooling around, either. Those attempting the genocide of the people of Tempran Silver would be given no quarter.

The railgun hammered ahead of Rivka. Return fire punched down the stairwell.

"Launch it now!" someone called from above.

Red fired again and tried to move, but the return fire was too intense.

We need the warriors right now. Soldiers on the roof are

getting ready to launch the balloon. I don't know what it looks like, but we need our people to stop this. It's our only chance.

Accelerating to Mach Five, Clodagh replied.

"Red, the ship is inbound," Rivka shouted up the stairs.

"Standing by," Red called back. He fired sporadically, then unleashed a long stream in rapid-fire mode.

Rivka climbed up to where she could see. He tried to hold her back with his foot, but she jumped over his leg. Above, the balloon lifted above the view through the blasted door.

"Holy fuck!" She grabbed Red by his body armor and pulled him back. "We have to get out of the impact area."

Red resisted, but the soldiers on the roof kept firing down the stairs. The bodyguard recoiled from impacts on his chest protection.

"We can't get to the roof. Tactical retrograde," Red snapped.

"Run for your lives!" Rivka shouted while scrambling down the stairs and jumping through the hole where the door used to be.

Tex picked up the injured woman, who screamed in pain and passed out. He bolted through the door to the stairwell that led down. Dennicron and Billi Jane waited since the Magistrate had hesitated until Red joined them.

"Go!" he roared angrily.

We see it. Intercepting the balloon now. Crap! We ripped through it.

A *ka-thump* rocked the building, and flames shot down the steps from the roof.

Red cried out in pain. Dennicron and Billi Jane wrapped themselves around the Magistrate in the doorway to the stairs. A low rumble vibrated the building, rippling outward.

"Too late," Rivka muttered, but no one could hear her. She ducked her head and waited for the building to come down.

CHAPTER TWENTY

***Wyatt Earp*, above the City**

The balloon appeared an instant before *Wyatt Earp* ran into it and tore through it.

Clodagh braced herself, but the damage was done. *Wyatt Earp* jerked to a stop and started to back up to deploy Cole and his warriors, who were waiting on the cargo ramp.

They screamed in unison, and the sound echoed through the ship.

A fireball filled the view behind the ship. "Go, go!" Clodagh yelled, but Clevarious had already taken over. The ship banked hard and accelerated to Mach Ten to race around the explosion and the expanding fireball.

The entire block beneath the detonation was masked by flame and smoke.

Clodagh could only hang on.

The ramp closed. The gravitic shields were still in place, protecting the ship.

The ship continued angling until it intersected with fire

heading away from the city. It flew through the flames, instantly extinguishing the fireball.

The atmosphere below burned, but the intensity of the fire was already lightening.

"Back to the building. Cole, prepare to dig through the rubble to find the Magistrate."

The ship slowly approached through the smoke until the air cleared, showing that the buildings still stood.

"We did it," Clodagh said. "But what did we do?"

"The detonation was ill-timed," Clevarious replied. "And too low for the full impact. Plus, I'm happy to report that our speed created the predicted troughs that helped eliminate the cascade effect. The first is already burning itself out."

Magistrate, are you there? Clodagh asked.

Clevarious moved the ship over top of the tallest building. "Cole, go find our people."

We're here. Top floor. Red's hurt. We need pickup right now.

Cole! Hurry up! Clodagh knew they couldn't hurry. The building could be unstable. They weren't sure how much damage had been done by the explosion and the follow-on burn.

Already on the roof. Moving down the stairs, Cole reported.

Rivka held Red in her arms. His body armor had melted into his skin. His railgun was a mess of fused parts, or everything that wasn't a base metal.

"He blocked the blast coming down the stairs with his body."

"Two thousand degrees," Dennicron said.

Red struggled to draw each breath. He teetered on the edge of consciousness. They all heard someone wearing powered armor pounding down the stairs.

"Magistrate?" Cole called from the other side of the hole.

"Cole! We're down the hallway."

"I can't get through. Stand by."

Rivka nodded at Dennicron. "Help him open that door. We can probably unbolt it now."

Dennicron hurried away.

I'm at the bottom. You're not coming, but I don't think the injured lady can handle me coming back up the stairs, Tex reported.

Rivka didn't bother to recommend the elevator since the power was out. She didn't know why, but it suggested the damage was more widespread than just the burn damage at the top of the building.

Go outside and wait. If the van is operational, take it back to the spaceport. We'll meet you there. Rivka sighed. There was more to do. *Clodagh, how's the city?*

Intact, Magistrate. The detonation didn't create the effect they wanted. Some of the atmosphere burned, but it didn't continue. Damage is localized.

We need to get on the horn and stop the evacuation by my order. The evacuation is canceled, and all ships are grounded. Passengers are to return to their homes.

I'll relay the message.

Rivka winced at the grind and scream when the door to the roof was opened using the combined efforts of powered combat armor and the SI mobility platforms.

A warrior clumped down the hallway toward them.

"I'll take him back to the ship, Magistrate," Cole offered.

"No, I've got him." Rivka stood and let Red fall over her shoulder. His injuries were on his back. She could carry him without exacerbating his wounds.

Inbound. Lower the cargo ramp, Rivka directed.

It's already down. Bring them aboard, Clodagh replied. *Tyler's waiting.*

Up the twisted stairs, where they found *Wyatt Earp* hovering close to the roof door. They stepped across the scorched and warped roof panels and climbed into the ship. Tyler helped guide Red into the Pod-doc, then closed the lid and activated the system. It had a great deal of work to do.

"We have another injured. She broke something when Dennicron tried to clear the luxury yacht's ramp. We feel responsible," Rivka explained. "She's down on the ground."

"Clodagh, get us to the ground so we can intercept Tex."

"Coordinating now. Give me a minute."

Rivka paced. She had things to do, but there was nothing more important than getting their injured taken care of.

The ship lifted off the roof and corkscrewed between buildings to wedge into an intersection below. Tex ran aboard carrying a local woman.

"I'll take a look at her," Tyler said.

Tex gently deposited her into a chair near the Pod-doc and Tyler began his examination, checking her clavicles, shoulders, arms, and ribs. With the Pod-doc, he could fix her up in a matter of minutes. She had a broken rib and a dislocated shoulder.

"I'm going to wrap your rib cage to keep pressure on this rib." He pointed. "And then we're going to put that shoulder back into place."

He gave her a pain pill and a glass of water before doing anything else. He took his time putting the wrap in place to give the pill more time to work. He waited until her eyes dilated. "Sit up straight and give me your hand."

She whimpered while raising her hand. Tyler braced himself, smiled, pulled up, and pushed to drive the shoulder back into the socket.

Her eyes shot wide, but only for a moment. She sighed in relief and leaned back. Tyler put a mat on the deck and helped her lie down.

Tyler nodded to Rivka that all was on track.

Rivka tipped her chin at him and headed for the bridge. She had to prevent any more damage to Tempran Silver. She had two parties to an arbitration in which the leaders were in her brig or otherwise under investigation for fraud or other crimes against the people of Tempran Silver.

That didn't leave anyone in charge.

Rivka scowled. That meant she would have to put the pieces together.

Lindy met her in the corridor. Rivka stopped. "He'll be okay."

"What did he do?"

"What he always does. He protected me by putting his body between the fire and the rest of us. It burned him, but not as bad as it would have been without his ballistic protection. His body armor saved him."

"That's what it's supposed to do. Dery wasn't worried. Sounds like it looked worse than it was."

Rivka shook her head. "It was bad. Without the Pod-doc, he probably wouldn't have made it."

Lindy looked at the cargo bay. "Do you know how long he'll be in there?"

"Are you going to chew his ass?"

"Probably." Lindy smiled. "I feel numb. Maybe we all should have died. We weren't supposed to be here when that thing went off."

"That's the truth. It's not a very Magistrate thing to do, being in the midst of the start of a civil war."

Lindy put her hand on the Magistrate's shoulder. "Maybe not, but it's a very Rivka thing to do, and Red, too. When can we get some time off?"

"That is a good question, and I better chew Grainger's ass. We can't prosecute cases back to back to back. I think we're losing our edge." Rivka puffed out her cheeks and exhaled heavily.

"We're on edge, Magistrate. We shouldn't be getting our people hurt like this. It was supposed to be an arbitration. Force them to negotiate, accept some terms, and get back to work. Next time we get some time, Red and I want to go to Azfelius with Dery. The pilots want to go to Station 7 with their boyfriends. The SCAMPs need to go to Rorke's Drift. You and Tyler should go to some resort moon where you can't be contacted."

"Is that what I'm supposed to tell Grainger?" Rivka wondered. She waved off the answer before Lindy could give it. "It is what I'll tell him. I don't want to get our people killed because we're not sharp enough. You have my word. Now, let's finish this case so we can start relaxing."

"Do we ever relax?" Lindy snarked.

"You're going to put Bristle Hound on Azfelius and then tell him to relax? How about you go to a rifle range and shoot stuff?"

"That will be our challenge. Getting the faeries to build us a rifle range." Lindy waved. "I'm going to check on my husband. Why don't you go save the day, Magistrate, and if you want to leave the ship, please let me know. I'll go with you. Red will get mad if you go alone."

"We don't want that." Rivka waved over her shoulder as she continued to the bridge.

Clodagh moved out of the captain's chair the second Rivka arrived.

The Magistrate nodded. "Give me a planetwide broadcast." She stopped halfway into sitting down. "Why can we see the top of the buildings?"

"The fire burned off the lowest layer of pollutants," Clodagh replied.

"Controlled burn. Can we burn off the bad atmosphere? How much O2 is left? Clevarious! I need answers so I can make better proposals to whoever is left on this God-forsaken rock."

"Oxygen content has dropped to eighteen percent, which is the minimum needed to sustain life," the ship's SI replied.

"Track that. I bet it increases with a little breeze from the outer regions. We don't need atmospheric generators; we need big fans. I've heard the solution to pollution is dilution. And then, of course, not adding any additional pollutants to the air."

"We are taking continual readings of the air outside the ship."

Rivka smiled. "Most excellent. What's the status of the evacuation?"

Clevarious replied. "Not a single ship had departed. The evacuation fleet is still on the ground."

"Civilian casualties from the device's detonation and stillborn atmo burn?"

"None known, but that doesn't mean there aren't any. Reporting mechanisms are not in place because of the evacuation."

Rivka reveled in the image on the main screen showing buildings rising on each side. The yellow soup was higher in the atmosphere, creating the impression of dawn, not twilight as had previously existed.

"Now you can give me a planetwide broadcast."

Clodagh pointed at her, then gave her the thumbs-up.

"People of Tempran Silver, this is Magistrate Rivka Anoa. The terrorist group that attempted to destroy the city and all the people within has been dealt with. Their device was prematurely detonated, leading to an explosion that did *not* result in a runaway atmospheric burn.

"Tempran Silver is safe for the moment, but this event has given us an opportunity to make things right for all the people: Labor, government, corporate, and their families. There is no reason to be contentious on either side of the problem. Those who have been misleading you are no longer in power. There will be new leadership on Tempran Silver. The mines will reopen, and the wealth therefrom will be a planetary asset, not just for one side.

"We will meet at the spaceport shortly, where I will bring the two sides together to hammer out the details for the way forward. We're going to get Tempran Silver back on its feet."

Rivka closed the channel.

"Go to the spaceport?" Clodagh asked.

Rivka nodded. She steepled her fingers and stared at the screen. "Dennicron, Chaz, Ankh, Erasmus, Sahved, Tex, and Billi Jane, meet me in the conference room right now, please. We have a planet to save." Rivka rose from the captain's chair but didn't go farther. "Clevarious, Ryleigh, Clodagh, thank you for driving the ship. You may very well have saved the people of this planet. Consider yourselves prime candidates for the Magistrate's Medal of Service."

Clodagh looked skeptical. "I've never heard of it."

Rivka laughed. "The very first recipient of it was Floyd, so you'll be in elite company. Seriously, though, I'll see if I can get you some extra pay or something. You deserve more than my gratitude."

"I don't think we do," Clodagh replied. "Your gratitude and understanding are enough for me. We have a home because of you."

Rivka tipped her chin to the chief engineer. "Station 7, Ryleigh? What are you and the others going to do there with your buff boyfriends?"

Ryleigh turned in her seat to face the Magistrate and deadpanned, "Unspeakable things." She spun back to face the screen.

Clodagh looked away.

Rivka raised her finger as if she wanted to make a point but couldn't come up with anything. Discretion made her head for the conference room instead.

The others were already assembling. Rivka took her

seat and waited. Ankh showed up about ten seconds later, which was timely for him.

"Ankh, I need the Singularity to calculate flight paths to create channels between the layers of the polluted atmosphere. Then we're going to light them up layer by layer. We're going to burn off as much of the pollution as we can get away with without driving the oxygen below eighteen percent.

"Then I want to use those ships to drag fresh air in behind them. I'm sure that will take some precise calculations, something the Singularity is uniquely suited for. As another task for the Singularity, I'll need an SI to manage this planet."

"Chrysanthemum has already volunteered for that task."

"You're sending your wife away?" Rivka blurted.

"No. She's going to take care of Tempran Silver to guarantee the Singularity's supply of bolarium six. We'll reunite when the operation is on track. A new SI will be installed at that time. We'll advertise on the Singularity's job board."

"A job board." Rivka smiled at Ankh, who stared at her with his usual blank expression. "Chrys will be the perfect addition. Ask her to be ready to go ashore as soon as we land. I want to introduce her to the people she'll be working with."

Ankh left the conference room.

"That was about ninety-five percent of what I needed done. Dennicron, Chaz, Tex, and Billi Jane, work with the Singularity to come up with those calculations. We'll put one of you on each ship to help guide them on their flight profiles and tasks. I expect *Wyatt Earp* will provide the detonation. What will we use?"

"That is the good news." Dennicron beamed. "We've developed an exploding plasma bomb that can be launched from our ion cannon. It'll be spectacular, but with the speed it'll travel, the calculations need to be down to the nanosecond. We'll be able to stay in one place and fire wherever we need to fire. The ion cannon has an intra-atmospheric range of hundreds of kilometers."

The SIs hurried out. That left Sahved at the table and Lindy leaning in the doorway.

"How is Red doing?" Rivka asked.

"It'll be a while, but the Pod-doc is whirring and blinking like it's supposed to. The other patient is resting comfortably. She's pretty doped up. Doc said he'll stuff her in the Pod-doc once Red recovers."

Rivka nodded. She stared at the table, scowling. "Those fuckers. They tried to blow up the planet and all the good people on it, including us. At least they had the decency to kill themselves while doing it."

"Not Zagreb," Sahved offered.

"*Zagreb*. Genocide is most assuredly a capital crime. Should I execute him?"

Sahved held up his hands. "Don't put that on me, Magistrate. That's your determination, and it has be to the council's—if they review it. I doubt Zagreb has any friends, so it'll probably languish in obscurity and never be reviewed."

"Of course, you're right, Sahved. I'll send Zagreb to Jhiordaan with a life sentence. I've heard that I'm the judge, jury, and executioner, but we'll leave that executioner part for when people shoot at me first. Like those soldiers who launched the balloon. Red was in their face and forced them to launch prematurely. They were going to kill their own people, too. How sordid is that?"

"Maybe they didn't know what the balloon would do. It doesn't seem like they had a plan to extricate themselves."

"Zagreb, hanging his people out to dry. They're going to love him on Jhiordaan."

Clevarious came over the speaker. "We're landing next to the yacht, *Tempran Minerals*."

"Time to go," Rivka said.

Lindy ushered her into the corridor. Floyd bounded up to them.

Go? the wombat asked.

"No, little girl. There's nothing green out there for you to eat, but you know what? When we're finished here, we're going to Azfelius. Would you like that?"

Plant planet! Yeah!

"Yes, the plant planet. It's one big buffet to you. You've lost all kinds of weight, so I don't need you gorging while you're there."

Fat wombat is happy wombat.

"That's debatable, little girl. We have to go do this thing. Wait here. Hopefully, it won't take too long."

Rivka and Lindy found their way to the airlock, where Chrysanthemum waited for them. She carried nothing, though she was going to remain on the planet for as long as it took to restore the bolarium shipments.

"No extra clothes?"

"I'll buy and wear what the locals wear. It will help them accept me."

"Good plan."

Lindy stepped in first, then the Magistrate. Chrys joined them and cycled the airlock. Lindy and Rivka made faces as they put their breathing masks on.

"It'll be too soon if we never have to wear these things again," Rivka groused.

They stepped out into air that was clearer than expected. Rivka took off her mask and immediately started coughing. She held her breath until she could get her mask back on. "Looks can be deceiving. The air is still crap."

Sahved shook his head. "I could have told you that."

"Sorry. I should have asked." Rivka wondered why she relied less on Sahved's counsel than she could have. Was it his age or lack of experience? Was it how he came across as doofy sometimes? Maybe too often, but he was astute. He saw things she didn't. "Sahved, how do we continue the negotiations when we have no one left on either side of the issue?"

"Appoint someone to accept whatever you tell them. I don't think there is any need for a negotiation. It is arbitration, and you've heard all the arguments. Dictate the decision and make them responsible for carrying it out."

Rivka smiled. "Sahved, that was the answer I came to."

"Then why did you ask?"

"To confirm what I thought. You're one of us, Sahved."

The lanky Yemilorian grinned as he bowed deeply.

The group continued up the ramp and into the luxury yacht. The two guards were no longer under the broken clear screen, although it was where they had left it.

Various individuals strolled the corridors. Rivka recognized them from the crowd she had encountered on her second time aboard. They were the so-called elite of the labor team.

In the ship's main space, she found the majority of the passengers squeezed in and uncomfortable.

"When are we taking off?" someone boldly asked from the anonymity of the crowd.

"This ship is grounded. The evacuation is canceled as the threat has been eliminated. I need you to return to your homes and await further instructions."

"How about you suck my ass?" the bold person blurted.

"That one," Sahved ducked to keep from hitting his head on the ceiling. He pointed at someone he could easily see over the mass of heads.

Lindy waded in, and the crowd parted. No one was willing to stand up for the bigmouth. "Wait!" he cried as Lindy dragged him into the open.

"Should I beat him until he learns some respect?" Lindy said in a voice that sounded like a young girl's to insult the loudmouth's manliness.

He was appropriately cowed once he found himself on his own.

"What's your name, and what do you do?"

"I am Septran, general foreman working the underground. With the collapse, I'm just a nobody, I guess."

Rivka offered her hand. "Although no one is going to suck your ass, they may listen when you talk about the mine because few, if any, know it better than you."

"You got that right."

"I'm Magistrate Rivka Anoa, and this is Chrysanthemum," Rivka gestured at the SCAMP. "She will be the Federation's Special Representative to oversee the rebuilding of your city and your planet. The previous two parties to the negotiations have been thrown in jail, killed, or charged with crimes, so you're going to be it. I need a plan to restore production of bolarium."

"The mine has collapsed," Septran stated as if that answer would end the conversation.

"I know. You're going to figure out how to get it producing again. The good news is that you have the full support of all the miners and their equipment. It is all at your command. Plus, you'll have as much engineering and technical help as you want from the Singularity."

"All of the miners work for me?"

"Effective immediately, but you can be replaced if you do wrong by them."

He frowned. "Who's the Singularity?"

"Chrys is a member. It's the race of sentient intelligences. They have a great deal of technical knowledge, as in, they know about everything there is to know."

"They know everything," he snapped. "Sounds like the ones who used to be in charge. They couldn't dig cling-ons out of their own asses."

"Chrys is different. She'll support you without getting in your way. Whether you sink a new shaft or look for new deposits, you decide, but you need to get the supply train rolling. There's a huge demand for bolarium six. You'll need to employ air scrubbers in your crushing and processing operation. We're going to clear the air over the city. You'll need to keep it clear."

"You can do that?"

"We've learned a thing or two during our time here. Yes, we can do that. We're making the calculations now."

"You can do that?" he repeated.

"Pick some trusted people and look at a plan. I don't want to hear no for an answer. Figure it out. Cost is not a consideration. Time is of the essence."

"How can cost not be a consideration? This is going to be expensive. We might need some new equipment."

"Turns out the planetary resources are extensive. They've been frozen and will be allocated as Chrys sees fit. Defend your requests well. Now, get to work. Remember, time is of the essence."

"I was nobody until five minutes ago. This is going to take some time to get my head wrapped around." The man looked less confident than he previously had.

"You weren't nobody. You were a mine foreman without a mine to work. Now the mine is yours to establish and exploit, but this time, do it without destroying your planet. That's not too much to ask, is it?"

He laughed. "It's what we've been asking for for ten years."

"So, you've been thinking about it for ten years. That was the time for complaining. Now it's time for action," Rivka explained. "Take my hand. Seal the deal."

He shook her hand, wearing a wry smile. In his mind, he was optimistic. He'd been a dreamer. It was like winning the lottery. "I'm sorry, Magistrate, for telling you to suck my ass."

Rivka laughed. "If that's the worst thing I hear, today is a pretty good day."

Chrys offered, "I'll stay behind. Rally the team, as it may be. I'll find a ride to the government-corporate headquarters. They have the computers, so I'll complete my integration with them at that time. The Singularity has everyone locked out of them, so there's no risk."

"Find Galwyn, and tell him he's our point of contact."

"You pick Galwyn despite him being morally bankrupt?" Chrys wondered.

"I forgot about that. No. Fuck that guy. Pick someone else."

"I'll find someone suitable. There's no rush since the government-corporate entity handled sales, and we won't have anything to sell for a while. Don't worry, Magistrate. I'll get it under control. Station 11 was a challenge since people's loyalties were all over the place. When they worked toward the same goal, it was amazing to see how much better the station ran."

Rivka smiled. "Then we're out of here. We're going to have to do some fancy flying, I figure. I look forward to that. You take care of people on the ground, and we'll take care of the sky. We'll start higher up in the atmosphere so we don't blow out any windows. We may be able to leave the lower layers to dissipate. Unite these good people behind a new planet and new leadership."

She leaned close. "Are you going to be okay without Ankh and Erasmus?"

"Of course. Why wouldn't I be?"

"You're still a newlywed by my calculations."

Chrys activated her good humor subroutine. "And we will always be. I will be in constant contact with them. We'll use the instantaneous intergalactic communications terminal. They've deployed one on a drone. I'll install it in my office after you've departed."

"Of course they have. I should have figured they were a couple steps ahead of me."

Chrys didn't dignify that with an answer.

"Anything else we need to do, Sahved?" Rivka asked.

"Your methodology defies logic, Magistrate. I simply accept that it works. I would not have chosen the mouthy man."

"We'll see. You know the saying, Sahved. The jury is still out."

He nodded.

Rivka twirled her finger. "Time to go, people."

When they reached the ship, Rivka tossed her mask aside. "Last time for that nasty thing." She strutted out of the airlock and found Ankh waiting for her.

He spoke with Erasmus's voice. "This mission should not have turned out as it did. My compliments, Magistrate."

"Case, Erasmus. It was a case, and not even that. It was an arbitration. I hope Billi Jane and Tex don't feel bad. This case was a mess. Pure chaos. It took an intervention since no amount of negotiating was going to resolve it. Sometimes it takes a Magistrate's heavy hand to bring the parties in line."

"But they tried to destroy the planet and everyone on it."

"At least the city and access to the bolarium, but they didn't destroy it. They failed because we stayed on top of the evil they would do. I never wanted this case, Erasmus. Red suggested we let them destroy each other. But you need bolarium six in your factory. The Federation needs its planets not to be embroiled in civil wars. We did what we had to to keep that from happening, and now we're going one step farther. We're going to clean up their mess and put them back on track to be a healthy and productive society."

"The calculations are finished, Magistrate. The fleet can take off whenever you're ready."

"That's the best thing I've heard all day. Clevarious, you are the fleet commander. Give them their marching orders. Deploy the fleet!"

CHAPTER TWENTY-ONE

<u>Tempran Silver</u>

Rivka strolled to the bridge.

Lindy had gone to the cargo bay to check on Red.

Sahved followed Rivka.

Clodagh stood. "Stay there," Rivka told her. "I'm just an observer for this."

It took a few minutes to get the ships airborne. They complained about low fuel, passengers, maintenance, and just about everything, but the SIs confirmed that the ships were good to fly. Those who hadn't disembarked had a front-row seat for the maneuvers that would clear the atmosphere.

Wyatt Earp took the center position. The other ships flew close by in a V formation like wild geese flying south for the winter.

They accelerated, and the sound of their engines tore at the sky and the ground below. Their wakes created a channel into which *Wyatt Earp* launched a plasma bomb from the ion cannon, and the explosion started a fire that burned a layer away. The ships flew out of the pollution and descended three hundred meters to do it again.

Twenty times they repeated the exercise, clearing layer after layer of pollution.

"Oxygen is holding steady at eighteen percent. Recommend we cease the bombing," Clevarious stated.

"Concur," Rivka agreed. She wasn't in a position to overrule the SIs when it came to calculated risks. "Fly through the remaining layers and see if we can spread them out a little. Maybe drag good air into the city."

The ships made three passes from outside the city through the lower layers. It didn't achieve the desired effect.

"No change," Clevarious reported.

"Put the fleet on the ground and send the passengers home. Put us in orbit, please. I'll be in my quarters once I see how Red is."

Rivka left the bridge, not as happy as she felt she should have been. They'd won. She wasn't ready to close the case yet, but she was close. She only needed to talk to Grainger.

She found Red climbing out of the Pod-doc. His gear was in tatters. Tyler and Lindy cleaned it out before putting the local in to repair her rib and make final adjustments to her shoulder.

"How are you, big guy?" Rivka moved close and helped Lindy guide him to a chair.

"That hurt like the flames of Hell were calling me down. No more fires, Magistrate. That was bad. The worst I've ever been hurt."

"That sucked. We would have witnessed the death of a planet had it not been for *Wyatt Earp*."

"Hooray for the most badass ship in the Federation."

"*War Axe* might dispute that, but I'm happy with our home. And I'm happy with you guys. I couldn't have surrounded myself with better people. You can't get bigger, Red. I carried your big ass, and it took everything I had."

"You need to hit the gym more often, Magistrate. You've been slacking," Red muttered. "I'm pretty tired. Request permission to hit the rack."

"You don't need my permission to rest after nearly dying. I won't be leaving the ship anytime soon, Red. I'm calling Grainger next to see if we can pull the chocks, declare victory, and get the fuck out of here."

"What about our passenger?" Lindy nodded at the Pod-doc, where Tyler was tinkering with the controls.

"We'll drop her off on our way out. Gating from inside the atmosphere means we don't have to delay."

Lindy draped Red's arm over her shoulder so she could help him stand. As they slowly walked away, Dery appeared and flew close to his dad. Red smiled at the boy.

Rivka returned to her quarters, sat at her desk, and brought up the hologrid.

"C, connect me to Grainger."

He answered right away. "What is that, two in a row where you called me at a decent hour and not in the middle of the night?"

"A fluke, I assure you. I'll try harder next time to inconvenience you as much as possible. Which is why I called. This case is done. Chrys is working to get the mining back on track. We have a couple perps we'll stick on the next prison ship we find, and we've done an initial scrub on the atmosphere, thanks to flying fast and hard. We could still use one atmospheric generator if you can rustle one up for us."

"Are you calling the case closed? That's good since we have a new case that I think you'll find interesting."

"No. I'm putting my foot down. We're taking two weeks off. We'll pick up our next case at the end of that. It's non-negotiable, Grainger. We're losing our edge. This one was close. We almost got Red killed, and we were almost in the middle of a conflagration that could have killed everyone on Tempran Silver. It was way too close. We need to be a little sharper, and that means time off."

"I'm sure Frenzik can wait," Grainger said with a shrug. "Take your time. He'll probably be there when you get back."

"You suck." Rivka leaned back. She wanted nothing more than to put the cuffs on Frenzik, wipe that smug look off his face, and drag him off to Jhiordaan. "White-collar crime, right? Why don't you put Bustamove on it?"

"Because it's no longer what we would consider white collar. Racketeering and murder. People are disappearing and getting replaced by Rising Sun employees."

"We just went through that on Tempran Silver. If it looks like they're offing the leadership and replacing them with their own people, they are. The locals on Albion love him, which means it has to be on one of the other planets in the Barrier Nebula."

"It is. The SI you put on Ypswich is missing, too."

Rivka chewed on her lip. "Two weeks, Grainger. We need two weeks off. Then we'll go deal with Frenzik and his minions. We'll turn the Singularity loose on them right now to make sure Rising Sun is contained. We don't want them growing legs and getting outside the Barrier Nebula."

"Two weeks, Rivka. I expect you'll be out of contact?"

"We'll be off the grid. You can email information as it changes. I'll get caught up every now and then because I can't stay away, but I have to give my people time off. We're going to get someone killed if we don't get a refresh. This isn't optional. I'd love to go hammer on Frenzik right now, but no can do. I'm a bit burned out and can't risk it."

"I hear you. Two weeks. Enjoy your time away. Then get yourselves to the Barrier Nebula. Case file will be in your inbox."

Tyler walked in, and Rivka dropped the hologrid.

"Do we get our time off?" he asked.

"Even with the threats, yes. Seems like Frenzik has crossed the line and we get to go after him."

"Right now?"

"No. We're taking two weeks." She sighed, moved to the couch, and sighed again. "What do you want to do?"

"You'd think that I would think about it, but I didn't. No thinking the thoughts I shoulda thunk."

"Pleasure moon. Sun. Pools. Spa. Golf. Sex. You know, the usual."

"I guess I could be up for a round of golf." Tyler sat next to Rivka on the couch. "What about the rest of the crew?"

"Milk run," Rivka replied.

"Sometimes you speak in tongues. I have no idea what you're saying."

"It means we'll fly to Azfelius, then to Station 7, then to Rorke's Drift, then to wherever Clodagh wants to go, and finally to the Venus pleasure moon orbiting Cygnus VI.

Clevarious, can you get us reservations there, please? And plot the courses, starting with dropping off the local once her injuries are repaired."

"It would be my pleasure to help the august crew of *Wyatt Earp* prepare for their pleasure," the SI replied.

Rivka's mouth twisted around. "What would *you* like to do for rest and recreation, C?"

"I would like to borrow Chaz's amulet once he is back in his SCAMP body so I can go on a walkabout. Say, of Station 7?"

"You want to party with the pilots? Are you sure you're up for that?"

"We shall see, should you grant my request."

"I shall, Master C. That means we go to Rorke's Drift first. Who's going to fly the boat?"

"Erasmus has agreed to take over flight duties."

"Ankh and Erasmus are going to stay on board?" Rivka laughed. "Belay that. A ship devoid of the insanity and chaos of its crew would be *their* idea of a vacation."

"This is where their laboratory is and where the embassy resides. Ankh will watch over Wenceslaus. Floyd will go with Dery, and Tiny Man Titan will join Clodagh, Alant, and Alanna. Is there anything else, Magistrate? You should start enjoying your downtime."

Rivka nodded. "After a short nap. Let me know when we're at Venus." Rivka pushed Tyler to the end of the couch so she could stretch out with her head in his lap. "You said you'd be up for a round of golf. I ought to kick your ass."

THE END

JUDGE, JURY, & EXECUTIONER, BOOK 18

If you liked this book, please leave a review. I love reviews since they tell other readers that this book is worth their time and money. I hope you feel that way now that you've finished the latest installment. Please drop me a line and let me know you like Rivka's adventures and want them to continue. This is my new favorite series. I hope you agree.

Don't stop now! Keep turning the pages as Craig hits his *Author Notes* with thoughts about this book and the good stuff that happens in the *Kurtherian Gambit* Universe.

Your favorite legal eagle will return in JJE20, FRENZIK

AUTHOR NOTES - CRAIG MARTELLE

WRITTEN JULY 2023

I wrote JJE18, *The Mob*, in February. We put it through the QC process, and all went well. It launched. Life was good. And then I got RSV, a new respiratory virus that was harsh on little kids and old people. I caught Covid in July 2022. I had a racking cough, and I was tired all the time, but I fared okay. In November, I caught the flu and survived that after a few miserable days. But RSV... I ended up in the Intensive Care Unit for two days. It was bad.

That put me behind but also ahead. After tanks of oxygen, nebulizers, and antibiotics, they juiced me on a mega load of prednisone for two full weeks. Last time I took prednisone, it made me feel awful, but not this time! It was just what the doctor ordered. I wrote a whole book (almost) over those two weeks. That put me ahead for the year.

Torch the Sky, on the other hand, was in process for a

couple weeks before I headed to London for a two-day show with my friends from the Self-Publishing Formula and then for four days in Palma de Mallorca for a conference there. Both events were exceptional but took one hundred percent of my attention. I had no time to write, but that's okay. The time I gained in March was invested in good conversations to keep my author business moving forward.

We arrived home on June 30th, and I was promptly back in the saddle.

By July 5th, my wife was on her way to Miami for advanced yoga teacher training to complete her five-hundred-hour certification, so I got to ride solo for five weeks. That meant just me and Stanley.

The mosquitoes were so bad that even Stanley didn't want to be outside, and this is the time of year when he loves being outside. He *is* a dog, after all. In any case, we are making do. When I wrote this, I still had four weeks left of being home alone. I'm not sure what the odds are of me turning feral before her return, but currently, they are in my favor.

In this book, I wanted to explore the dichotomy of two parties threatening the exact same dire action to achieve a different goal. It sounds moronic, but it happens more often than you realize because people shape their arguments in ways to make the other "side" look like the one intent on delivering the big hammer of pain. Take a closer look, and you may see that no one has your best interests at heart. Most people are out for themselves. It's a shame to see modern society that way, but we have to look out for ourselves as well.

In any case, that's the extent of my political commentary. I leave it to you to ask better questions of those who portend to represent you and do right by you. We don't have a Rivka in our lives, only on these pages.

My AFib returned most ingloriously this spring with a high-stress event, and then when I was in Mallorca, my friend James Blatch and I played nine holes. It was hot, but we had a cart and plenty of water. That didn't matter. My AFib rocketed back, and the attack lasted eight hours. I take a lot of medication to keep my heartbeat under control, so it didn't hit one hundred eighty beats per minutes, but it was up there, hovering between one hundred ten and one hundred thirty for eight hours.

Because of RSV, the AFib return, and the challenge of doing physical activities besides walking on a nice day, I'm going to pull back from doing in-person events in 2024. We'll see how that serves me. I will travel very little for the rest of this year–one trip to Vegas and then one trip to Pittsburgh. Both of those are in first class, so the stress should be minimal.

Next year, I'm committed to the Superstars Writing Seminar in Colorado Springs in February. We'll see if I go to GaryCon for the fiftieth anniversary of the publication of Dungeons & Dragons in March, although I'm leaning away from that. Then the Vegas show in November. That is minimal travel. I hope it helps my physical well-being.

But next! Next is *Frenzik*. This one will have a lot more action, a true run-and-gun thrill ride through the Magistrate's universe.

Until then, lots of stories to tell. Lots of characters to bring to life.

Peace, fellow humans.

Please join my newsletter (craigmartelle.com—please, please, please sign up!), or you can follow me on Facebook.

If you liked this story, you might like some of my other books. You can join my mailing list by dropping by my website craigmartelle.com, or if you have any comments, shoot me a note at craig@craigmartelle.com. I am always happy to hear from people who've read my work. I try to answer every email I receive.

If you liked the story, please write a short review for me on Amazon. I greatly appreciate any kind words; even one or two sentences go a long way. The number of reviews an eBook receives greatly improves how well an eBook does on Amazon.

Amazon—https://www.amazon.com/author/craigmartelle

BookBub—https://www.bookbub.com/authors/craig-martelle

Facebook—www.facebook.com/authorcraigmartelle

In case you missed it before, my web page—https://craigmartelle.com

That's it. Break's over, back to writing the next book.

OTHER SERIES BY CRAIG MARTELLE

#—available in audio, too

Terry Henry Walton Chronicles (#) (co-written with Michael Anderle)—a post-apocalyptic paranormal adventure

Gateway to the Universe (#) (co-written with Justin Sloan & Michael Anderle)—this book transitions the characters from the Terry Henry Walton Chronicles to the Bad Company

The Bad Company (#) (co-written with Michael Anderle)—a military science fiction space opera

Judge, Jury, & Executioner (#)—a space opera adventure legal thriller

Shadow Vanguard—a Tom Dublin space adventure series

Superdreadnought (#)—an AI military space opera

Metal Legion (#)—a military space opera

The Free Trader (#)—a young adult science fiction action-adventure

Cygnus Space Opera (#)—a young adult space opera (set in the Free Trader universe)

Darklanding (#) (co-written with Scott Moon)—a space western

Mystically Engineered (co-written with Valerie Emerson)—mystics, dragons, & spaceships

Metamorphosis Alpha—stories from the world's first science fiction RPG

The Expanding Universe—science fiction anthologies

Krimson Empire (co-written with Julia Huni)—a galactic race for justice

Zenophobia (#) (co-written with Brad Torgersen)—a space archaeological adventure

Battleship Leviathan (#)– a military sci-fi spectacle published by Aethon Books

Glory (co-written with Ira Heinichen)—hard-hitting military sci-fi

Black Heart of the Dragon God (co-written with Jean Rabe)—a sword & sorcery novel

End Times Alaska (#)—a post-apocalyptic survivalist adventure published by Permuted Press

Nightwalker (a Frank Roderus series)—A post-apocalyptic Western adventure

End Days (#) (co-written with E.E. Isherwood)—a post-apocalyptic adventure

Successful Indie Author (#)—a nonfiction series to help self-published authors

Monster Case Files (co-written with Kathryn Hearst)—A Warner twins mystery adventure

Rick Banik (#)—Spy & terrorism action-adventure

Ian Bragg Thrillers (#)—a hitman with a conscience

Not Enough (co-written with Eden Wolfe)—A coming-of-age contemporary fantasy

Published exclusively by Craig Martelle, Inc

The Dragon's Call by Angelique Anderson & Craig A. Price, Jr.—an epic fantasy quest

A Couples Travels—a nonfiction travel series

Love-Haight Case Files by Jean Rabe & Donald J. Bingle—the dead/undead have rights, too, a supernatural legal thriller

Mischief Maker by Bruce Nesmith—the creator of Elder Scrolls V: Skyrim brings you Loki in the modern day, staying true to Norse Mythology (not a superhero version)

Mark of the Assassins by Landri Johnson—a coming-of-age fantasy.

For a complete list of Craig's books, stop by his website—https://craigmartelle.com

CONNECT WITH THE AUTHORS

Craig Martelle Social

Website & Newsletter:
http://www.craigmartelle.com

Facebook:
https://www.facebook.com/AuthorCraigMartelle/

Michael Anderle Social

Website: http://lmbpn.com

Email List: https://michael.beehiiv.com/

https://www.facebook.com/LMBPNPublishing

https://twitter.com/MichaelAnderle

https://www.instagram.com/lmbpn_publishing/

https://www.bookbub.com/authors/michael-anderle

BOOKS BY MICHAEL ANDERLE

Sign up for the LMBPN email list to be notified of new releases and special deals!

https://lmbpn.com/email/

For a complete list of books by Michael Anderle, please visit:

www.lmbpn.com/ma-books/